THE WARS OF THE ROSES!

GAVIN THOMSON

MMXX

THIS BOOK BELONGS TO

_____

For John and Sebastian

This book is a work of fiction.
Any similarity to actual persons,
living or dead, or actual events,
is purely coincidental and confined
to the imagination of the reader!

1   Reputations and rosettes!

2   Morning chorus!

3   Bonfires, beekeeping and muck spreading!

4   Forest fires, earthquakes and landslides!

5   Roses are red, chocolates are red!

6   Secret service and preparation for war!

7   Flooding and fuelling the feud!

8   War and peace!

9   Peace and harmony and two doors!

1
Reputations and rosettes!

"Welcome to the annual summer fete award ceremony," announces Lady Margaret Beaufort in a voice so plummy, one would swear that she had swallowed a handful of ripe purple plums just before speaking. She taps the microphone to ensure that it is working after noting several members of the audience cupping their ears. "Can everyone hear me?" she asks, turning to the vicar who nods his head and mops his brow as the temperature rises inside the marquee on one of the hottest days of the year and after the most hotly contended competitions ever witnessed in the sleepy village of Rosewall.

Rosewall takes its name from the rose clad fortress walls encircling Woodville Castle that sits perched on Monitor's Mount and oversees the village. In full bloom, like today, the roses are a rainbow spectacle of red, white, blue, orange and pink, with scents that travel like an enticing tandoori, caressing the noses of the Rosewall inhabitants with the much-loved smell of summer.

Rosewall's annual fete is the yearly highlight, transforming the village green into an idyllic scene of food stalls and funfairs. Sometimes a spectacle of downpours and drenching, other times, as in this year, a Saharan scene of sweat-soaked shirts and sunstroke.

Children spend pocket money frivolously, all in the name of fun. Attempting to dislodge *shy* coconuts, throw the furthest welly, ride an uncoordinated bicycle, guess the number of sweets in a jar, have palms read by clairvoyants, drink copious amounts of lemonade, and hook yellow plastic ducks in the hope of an enormous pink teddy.

Adults, if not fulfilling their rota commitment or chaperoning toddlers, catch up on a year's gossip while devouring an undercooked sausage and downing watered-down beverages. Teams compete in the tug-of-war, jeered on by overzealous and over competitive support, culminating in the male rugby team taking on the female village folk, appearing to dominate then pulled to their knees in embarrassment and the high-pitched shrill of the victors. The award ceremony completes the day with the whole village piling into the marquee.

Lady Beaufort retrieves the half-moon tortoiseshell reading glasses nesting in her fabulous flowing grey locks and tethered to her neck with a yellow gold necklace, slightly tarnished through use. She positions the much-needed spectacles on the end of her nose, while she unbuttons the top button of her flowery silk blouse of emerald green and orange on a white background. Lady Beaufort fans her blouse back and forth to air her top half while shaking out her legs dressed in cream silk flared trousers and revealing cream patent leather Chanel slip-on shoes with distinctive shiny silver interlocking C-shapes.

"Wow!" she exclaims, shaking her head incredulously, "I think we should look into installing air conditioning next year," she declares, smiling and looking again at the vicar, who is nodding with a smirk any Instagrammer would be proud. "I feel like one of those iced buns," she continues, pointing to the bakery table. "Melting into the floor!"

The audience raises a titter, also nodding but wishing Lady Beaufort would proceed and put an end to this misery!

"We have four categories today," outlines Lady Beaufort, shuffling four sealed envelopes for all to see. "Best cake. Best pie. Best jam. And best rose. Judging this year has been exceptionally difficult with such a high standard, but I am sure or rather, I hope that you will agree with the decisions. So, without further ado, the winner of best cake goes to," she breaks the seal to remove the handwritten note and reads, "Mrs Stanley and her magnificent *cascading cake*."

Mrs Stanley holds her hand to her mouth, hiding her grin and her excitement, as she looks at her friends congratulating and clapping before she walks up to receive a golden rosette and a gift token for the local brasserie. "This is becoming quite a habit, Mrs Stanley," jokes Lady Beaufort, shaking hands. "This is the third year in a row. I assure you, ladies and gentlemen," she continues to joke, "the judging isn't fixed, and all tasting is blind, but thank you again, Mrs Stanley, for that twenty-pound note you slipped me earlier!"

Everyone laughs, fanning themselves with anything they can find, including A4 folded and stapled paper programmes which are fast becoming ineffective, saturated with sweat.

Mrs Stanley is the local librarian and an expert on all things Indian, having emigrated as a child from Bombay just before it renames to Mumbai. She looks the *coolest* person in the marquee heat, wrapped in a turquoise and gold sari, her jet-black hair tied back in a braided ponytail. Mrs Stanley is also an expert baker, especially ornate cakes, laced with Indian spices, tropical fruit and liqueurs to taste like nothing on earth. This year's entry, standing head and shoulders above the plethora of baked brilliance typical to a primary school bake sale is a cascading chocolate cake resembling an Amazonian waterfall. It has jungle-like trees and shrubs and an array of exotic animals such as brightly coloured parrots, swinging monkeys and constricting snakes. Everyone marvels how she can make chocolate look like water and waits patiently for judging to conclude to devour every slice, placing orders to keep Mrs Stanley busy until kingdom come.

"Best pie goes to," Lady Beaufort opens the second envelope to read, "Mr Hastings, for his outstanding *ocean liner pie.*"

Mr Hastings, the local fishmonger, who incidentally and unfortunately always smells of fish, combines the freshest fish and shellfish with layers of delicately blended vegetables and savoury sauces, disguised in a pastry topping to resemble a cruise liner complete with funnels, lifeboats and navigation decks. The pastry alone is a work of art and worthy of recognition. However, the exquisite taste of the filling forms a queue of eager hopefuls stretching the entire length of the marquee, delighted that the pie in its titanic white ceramic hull-shaped dish is large enough to feed everyone twice over. Ironically, today's heat would welcome a chilling iceberg.

Extending his theme, Mr Hastings wears a striped blue and white sailor's top and a sea captain's hat purchased online. He neglects to remove the sales tag on his top, displaying a forty per cent discount as he shakes hands and collects his golden rosette and a gift voucher for his own shop. You could not make it up if you tried.

Lady Beaufort turns up her nose as she sniffs her fingers after shaking hands, reeling from the smell of fish that everyone has grown to expect but struggles to accept. The vicar catches her, and they both smile, Lady Beaufort, turning two shades redder.

"Now to the award for best jam," continues Lady Beaufort, composing herself and gesturing to several tables laden with jars of all shapes, sizes and colour. "The category that always receives the most entries, and for which I have to say I *relish* most."

There is a general moan from the crowd in recognition of her pun, followed by another when Lady Beaufort adds, "and that always causes a judging jam because no one can decide which stands out best.

"But there can only be one winner," says Lady Beaufort, unphased by the audience's groaning response. She opens the third envelope and leans into the microphone to reveal in a loud whisper, "and the best jam goes to Miss Anne Neville and her *rainbow jam*."

A group of teenagers, congregating by the exit and fresh air, scream and shout Anne's name, jostling her to the front to collect her golden rosette and a gift voucher for afternoon tea at the luxury hotel, five minutes out of Rosewall. Typically, self-conscious, Anne stares at the floor, giggling with embarrassment.

Lady Beaufort is so impressed with the efforts of someone so young that she breaks rank to retrieve the winning tall clear jar and to hold up on stage for all to admire. "This is so clever and such a symphony of flavours," Lady Beaufort raves, indicating each layer. "Succulent red strawberry jam followed by a layer of tangy orange marmalade, followed by a layer of zesty lemon marmalade, followed by a green layer of tart, bitter gooseberry jam. Followed by a layer of sweet blueberry jam, followed by, and this is where it excels, a layer of indigo jam combining the distinctive flavour of Asian persimmon with British roadside blackberries. Delicious, to finish with a layer of purple rhubarb and plum jam, flavoured with a hint of juniper. Genius!"

While Anne passes around her gift voucher for all her friends to read with envy, Lady Beaufort sips from her water bottle, replacing it between the legs of the microphone stand. She takes a deep breath and launches into the finale. "Some may say that I have been saving the best to last while others may say that it always comes down to a two-horse race.

"There have been more entries than last year, and by that, I mean three. And I applaud young Henry Stafford for his sweet bouquet of hand-picked roses from his garden," she pauses to identify ten-year-old Henry and to encourage applause. "But once again it has come down to Rosewall's finest duelling florists - Rosemary Lancaster of Lancaster Blooms and her stunning array of Lancaster red roses, and Primrose York of York Blooms and her equally gorgeous York white roses."

•

Rosemary Lancaster and Primrose York are cousins once removed, relating to a common great grandfather, Edward Windsor, also a talented florist and prestigious plant agent for other florists and garden centres nationwide. He handed his florist to the next generation until eventually, it passed to Rosemary's father, Henry. Primrose's father, Richard, who rediscovered his love for flowers after becoming a successful plant agent for supermarkets, disputed Henry's sole inheritance, claiming entitlement to their grandfather's florist. The legal wrangling saw Henry and Richard swapping ownership, even sharing at one point, until it was easier and more cost-effective to divide the shop in half and create two independent florists. Henry began specialising in red flowers and Richard in white flowers, and roses became their signature, sparking the start of intense competition. They passed this rivalry onto Rosemary and Primrose, standing here today on far sides of the marquee, arms folded and looking at Lady Beaufort's envelope with piercing eyes as if attempting to mind-read its contents.

Rosemary personifies red with a fiery temperament, vibrant red long hair loosely tied with a large red bow, wearing a long flowing scarlet red summer dress, red pumps and the reddest of red lipstick to accentuate her Kardashian pout. Pinned to her chest is a striking silk red rose brooch, the biggest you will ever see.

By contrast, Primrose personifies white with a delicate demeanour, prim and proper, short pixie-cut blond hair with a white Alice band, a white knee-length summer dress, white sneakers, and a string of natural white pearls encircling her neck. Her lipstick, like Rosemary's, is red, but a pinker shade for a less pronounced pout and her silk white rose brooch is smaller and more refined.

Some think of Rosemary as the *naughty one* and Primrose as the *goody-goody*.

•

"Can someone remind me, who was the winner last year?" enquires Lady Beaufort, attempting to add more drama.

"That was me, Lady Beaufort," announces Rosemary in a loud voice and a side glance and smirk in Primrose's direction.

"Yes, yes. I remember now," responds Lady Beaufort, mischievously, "there were rumours of foul play! The York roses appeared to have black splatters which first appeared as black fly until after judging, further inspection revealed it to be black ink."

Rosemary says nothing, pursing her lips and dropping her gaze while Primrose shakes her head vigorously, muttering under breath.

"Anyhow," continues Lady Beaufort, lightening the mood and waving the remaining envelope like a lottery winner, "that was last year, and this is this year."

Rosemary and Primrose are beside themselves with anticipation, praying to a higher being. The audience shows allegiance, initially batting to and fro like a tennis crowd, before leaning towards Primrose in solidarity for last year's travesty.

"So, for the climax and the moment everyone has been waiting for, the winner of the best rose is," opening the envelope and slowing pulling out the notelet for extra effect, "Lancaster Blooms and her Lancaster red roses."

The audience gasps, expecting the reverse and turns to look at Rosemary with mouths open, stunned into silence by the result.

"Yes," screams Rosemary, skipping up to hug Lady Beaufort and to claim her golden rosette and a gift voucher for a weekend spa retreat of choice. "C'mon, you reds!" she chants, waving her clenched fist like a jubilant Liverpool supporter. She knows this will cement her reputation and increase sales as the go-to florist whenever anyone wishes to compose a declaration of love.

Primrose drops her head in disappointment, but ever gracious in defeat, she raises a smile and light applause towards Rosemary, mouthing congratulations, before turning to those around her for consolation.

"And on that bombshell," concludes Lady Beaufort, straightening herself after Rosemary's exuberant hug, "may I wish everyone a safe trip home and say how much I look forward to welcoming you back next year."

The marquee erupts into rapturous applause which follows outside as everyone makes a beeline for the exits in search of fresh air and escape from the torture of captivity. Even the red and white roses are wilting in the extreme heat.

Yellow vests take over the village green, collapsing gazebos and dismantling portable tables and chairs, spearing litter into black plastic bags and precariously building an empty cardboard box tribute to the coliseum after overfilling the designated wheelie bins. The *just too desperate,* queue for the portaloos, while defiant groups ignore the surrounding destruction, and continue to chat or to finish lukewarm beverages or both. They hold trays of earlier good ideas including thirsty pot plants, pork pies needing refrigeration, and second-hand books succouring and securing new homes. Children fall into two camps. Those that disobey, running off to play, and those that mope and moan, pleading to be carried home, energy coincidentally spent with pocket money.

Rosemary carries her golden rosette winning bouquet to her vermillion Citroen 2CV van, luckily parked in the shade alongside the ancient hedgerow. The doors have the Lancaster Blooms red rose logo, flamboyantly sign-written in gold typography, extending as a flowery device above the corrugated body. She attaches the rosette to the windscreen and climbs in to kickstart her two-horse carriage and return home.

Further along the hedgerow, Primrose deposits her bouquet into her white Vauxhall Combo van, tastefully decorated with the York Blooms logo sign-written in shiny silver and wrapping the entire back end. Dejected and exhausted after a day of hope and anti-climax, she turns the ignition and reverses to three-point turn towards the exit. Then who should be in front indicating left but Lancaster Blooms and its rear-facing slogan of *red roses scent with love.*

Primrose follows with gritted teeth, travelling the short distance through Rosewall towards Woodville Castle before turning into Woodville Watermill where she parks outside the left side, York Cottage while Rosemary parks outside the right side, Lancaster Cottage. Primrose and Rosemary are neighbours!

The cottages separate by a central watermill located on a stream that divides the property in half, covered at the front and running through to the rear where Rosemary grows her prize-winning red roses on one side. Primrose grows her past-winning white roses on the other.

•

Due to success selling flowers, even supplying tulips to the Dutch, Edward Windsor bought Woodville Castle with all its medieval history and grandeur. Similar to the florist shop, this passes through generations, ending with Rosemary and Primrose occupying separate sides of an over-sized high maintenance masterpiece which soon becomes a burden and a financial stretch too far. Rosemary and Primrose sell the castle to Heritage Trust and convert the watermill, perversely agreeing to live side by side despite their continued rivalry and retail independence. Primrose rationalises, "Sometimes one has to set aside one's differences for the sake of common sense and decency, Rosemary declaring, "We are rivals, not enemies, although sadly, we are neither friends. C'est la vie!"

•

Primrose turns the key in her white front door, and Rosemary opens her red front door. Not long later, Primrose and Rosemary are relaxing outside with a cup of tea on the central wooden deck extending back from the watermill and spanning the stream close to the cottages. They sit on either side of a six-foot-tall slatted wooden fence, each admiring their garden that stretches as far as the eye can see, Rosemary toasting her earlier success, Primrose licking her wounds.

"I'll beat you next year," Primrose shouts over the fence, looking proudly at her white roses, sparkling in the early evening sun. "Just you wait and see."

"Bring it on, Primrose," challenges Rosemary, confidently admiring her red velvet roses, smouldering in the fading sun. "Bring it on."

They both laugh uncontrollably, pouring another cup, separated by division but united in a common goal to create the perfect rose.

2
Morning chorus!

Another day is about to dawn in Woodville Watermill. Soft dew hangs from every possible point, blanketing both gardens in cleansing freshwater, revealing tracks of nocturnal lovers that meandered their way home to sleep away the fun and frolics of the night before. A neighbouring cat's pawprints walk across one side of the garden after a night on the tiles before leaping over the stream and traversing the other side to disappear over the enclosing high brick wall.

All is still for a brief moment like machinery halting when exchanging work shifts. Silence is both golden and deafening, lying motionless in anticipation of ensuing energy and illumination – a daily global phenomenon re-enacted since the beginning of time when the sun spawned life and routine into all-around.

It is a unique and magical period of each day, regardless of weather and the current season.

Then, without so much as a sign or a whisper, Watermill Stream prepares for another day of activity. Like an early walking horse that begins to trot, soon cantering to a gallop, things start slowly to overcome inertia until gathering a natural momentum, creating a scene in which any Wally can hide to be sought!

Rob and Bob are first to open their appropriately named *Early Birds Cafe*, both full of beans and chirping their familiar song with its catchy tune and simple lyrics more resembling *The Chuckle Brothers* than *The Beatles* as they bat back and forth *from me to you*.

We're The Early Birds, t'aint no surprises
Regular as clockwises
As the dawn sunrises
Seeking, coaxing, catching prizes
Squiggly, juicy, healthy sizes
To feed folk with paradises
We're *The Early Birds*, t'aint no surprises!

Their distinct sound of rap and rhythmic tweets awakens the garden diurnals from deep sleep to entertain a new day and all that it has to offer. Like a domestic dimmer switch, daylight brightens with every second, preparing for the warming sunlight to rise above the garden wall like a theatre spotlight identifying star players and the surrounding set especially given that today is another cloud-free summer's day.

Happy-go-lucky robin, Rob, is tiny when compared with Bob, his bigger blackbird colleague but he punches above his weight. Puffing out his bold chest to whistle the higher notes, Rob tweets single, treble, and quadruple beats like a Morse code translation. Bob intonates with calypso-like comedy, slapping his wings to mimic tom-tom drums, and warbling the lower notes like an operatic tenor. It is perfect harmony in action passed on from generation to generation, ad infinitum.

"What a beautiful day!" remarks Rob with a spring in his step. "Who needs to fly abroad when you've got weather like this?!"

"Absolutely, Rob," replies Bob. "*Staycation's* the new vacation!"

After pecking today's specials on a new piece of bark, Rob unpacks the latest delivery from Caterpillar Caterers. A stack of perfectly round nibbled leaves, ranging from sweet honeysuckle to English oak, all with stems intact. Bob wears his distinctive bright yellow apron to match his brilliant yellow beak and stokes the barbecue, fired and regulated by dragonfly, Dylan, lightly and heavily breathing fire. Bob prods and turns the variety of grubs, worms, seeds and fruit, freshly gathered by their wives, Bruna and Robyn, handed over moments before.

"Morning, all," announces Rob to his customers, turning the closed sign to open. "What can we get you?"

Rob and Robyn create wholesome wraps of cornucopia for the lengthening line, theatrically swashbuckling the leaf stems, taking care not to spill anything on their newly washed and ironed red waistcoats. Meanwhile, Bob and Bruna take turns on the barbecue, recording who eats what for bartering another time. All four sing and perform *The Early Birds* song, repeating its morning chorus for all to join, which one by one, they do when fuelled with savoury snacks.

Clarice, the starling, delivers her distinctive soprano shrill with startling effect in preparation for her midday operatic performance. Great tits, Dunny and Putz, join together with blue tit, Bozo, and yellow-bellied tit, Kwim, to perform their synchronised acapella version, while pluming, grooming and shaving customers in their shop, *The Barber Quartet*.

Cockney sparrows, Jack and Jimmy, clear their throats, shouting rather than singing the words like out of key and out of tune *karaokers*, replacing certain words and adding rhyming slang as they swagger around the bank, wheelbarrowing baskets and boxes between stalls. Hotel chambermaid hummingbirds, Harriet and Hettie, embellish with a melodic backtrack helping to disguise any imperfection, swaying side to side in unison and placing in front one foot after the other.

We're *The Early Birds*, t'aint no pork pies-es
Regular exercises
As the dawn sunrises
Seeking, coaxing appetise-es
Squiggly, juicy, drumstick thighs-es
to feed folk with blue eyes-es
We're *The Early Birds*, t'aint no pork pies-es!

Squirrel, Sam, and harvest mouse, Ella, run a vegetarian café next door to Early Birds, named, albeit unimaginatively, *Sam & Ella's cereal café*. Offering bespoke muesli, Sam is an expert on all things nuts, and Ella is a specialist on oats, wheat, bran and all things fibre. They offer gluten-free and allergy alternatives, all served in hazelnut shells with almond and oat cockroach milk, delivered fresh in handy-size peapods by Caterpillar Caterers.

"I'll have the morning chorus special, please, Sam," orders Tyrol, Sam's father, struggling to shift the weight after piling on the pounds over winter.

"I'll give you half a portion, Dad," responds Sam, smiling at Ella, "you know how calorific nuts are!"

Meanwhile, Fisher, a keen angler, businessman and the King of Watermill Stream, washes down the white marble plinth on which stands a tall marble column supporting a shiny brass sundial with its shadow display sharpening as the sunlight strengthens.

Delivery after delivery arrives, spearheaded by Queen Fishnette, Prince Fishin and Princess Fishelle. King Fisher positions the fresh catch of all shapes and sizes in the shade side of the plinth, taking care with the presentation before declaring *Fisher Mongers* open and ready for business. Now wearing blue aprons with central embroidered gold crowns, King Fisher starts serving, grinning and greeting with friendly banter, and catching up on local gossip.

"I hear that Lucky, the horseshoe bat ran out of luck last night!" tittle tattles chaffinch, Chav.

"How's that?" enquires King Fisher, repeating Chav's order to the kitchen.

"He overindulged down by the river, causing his radar to go awry," continues Chav, lifting her wing to hide her whisper. "So, he lost his bearings on the way home and crashed straight into a brick wall!"

Prince Fishin barbecues an aquatic assortment, fired and regulated by Dylan's baby brother, Thomas, for a more delicate flame. Some on skewers combining fruit and vegetables and others kept whole. All presented on woodchips with mushy peas and mint, a secret recipe handmade by Queen Fishnette and Princess Fishelle to ingredients again supplied by Caterpillar Caterers. They also offer their ever-popular and easy-to-hold battered tadpole lollipops, so good that they attract customers from further afield. King Fisher and family accompany the morning chorus while feeding customers on both land and stream.

•

King Fisher and Queen Fishnette have transformed Watermill Stream over the years, turning it into its now thriving commercial centre. As newlyweds, they inherited a tired and dirty stream, in chaos and disarray with unwanted sewage making it unstainable to life, and with inhabitants paying no respect to law nor order. The watermill compounded this being derelict and out of commission for many years until the broken watermill wheel renovates, and the passage of water unblocks to run free once more.

Rebranding ambitiously as *Riverbanks*, King Fisher and Queen Fishnette divide left and right banks into the right side for dwellings of all quality and distinction, and the left side for commercial and retail establishments, and they introduce the early morning market.

Watermill Stream extends out of Watermill, meandering a path to the far end of the property, flowing under a brick arch built into the enclosing wall then on into the meadow and beyond to join the river. Long grasses and overhanging trees occupy the far end, replaced by bushes, occasional bull rushes and water lilies approaching the mill. Riverbanks enjoys the advantages offered by the middle section, viewed as a natural centre and meeting point with a varied landscape, perfect for building a wide variety of natural architecture and efficient infrastructure.

No one operates or trades along the stream without permission. In return, there is regular maintenance, constant surveillance and a high standard of services. Anyone falling short must move further downstream, sometimes expelled altogether.

King Fisher and Queen Fishnette are firm but also fair as they do fish for their fair share of compliments!

•

Lord and Lady Bird, tailor and designer to anyone whose anyone In Riverbanks, entertain first customers in their recently redecorated shop, located in an imposing male bronze statue, nude and resplendent, newly installed under the overhanging willow and side-glancing Watermill Stream. Mirrors and sweeping staircases complement various wood panelling with a penthouse view through the statue eyes. Lennon, the long nose beetle, sits at the stairwell grand piano, classically playing to the morning chorus, adding a gentle touch of class and sophistication.

Lord Bird has a sense of tradition and expertise in bespoke tailoring. In contrast, Lady Bird has a passion and keen eye for the avant-garde, designing brightly coloured contemporary fashion and flamboyant millinery as the crowning glory to all outfits. Lord Bird measures stag beetle, Gordon for his wedding morning suit, set four weeks from now. Meanwhile, Lady Bird discusses fabric materials and patterns with the Scarab Prince beetle, who has flown in especially with his entourage, primarily to purchase a brand-new wardrobe for his forthcoming Arabic tour.

"Is sir planning to lose any weight before the wedding?" enquires Lord Bird, tape measuring Gordon's inside leg.

"My fiancé's put me on a strict diet," responds Gordon, breathing in with minimal effect, flexing his impressive muscles. "and I'm weightlifting every day at the gym!"

"What about this gorgeous metallic green silk, your highness," enthuses Lady Bird, draping the fabric over the Scarab Prince like a Roman toga, "woven and spun in the far east and exclusive to our salon?"

"I love it," agrees the Scarab Prince, admiring himself in the mirror. "I'll take four suits, six thawbs and three bathing robes."

Water boatman, Bryan, ferries passengers across Watermill Stream in an acorn cup strapped to his back, lead singing the morning chorus with his fellow ferrymen echoing every line like Venetian gondoliers. Bryan tiptoes as fast as he can from one side to the other to retain his prime position on the Riverbanks jetty and to stop his feet from getting wet!

"Cheers, Bryan," thanks woodlouse, Willy, disembarking, "I could have backstroked my way across but, however hard I thrash my legs, I always get swept along by the current and end up miles from my destination!"

"Sounds lousy!" jokes Bryan, assisting the next customer, Mike, the money spider, on his way to work in the bank.

White Admiral Nelson, commands a fleet of butterfly skippers, sailing an array of lily pads and fallen leaves up and down Watermill Stream, shipping supplies and larger loads. Including hordes of school children and commuters to the various collection and drop off points and to Riverbanks port, located in a naturally occurring inlet further downstream. Miraculously, there are no collisions, given the haphazard manner in which White Admiral Nelson and fellow skippers flutter their wings, tacking left and right, erratically while singing a sea shanty version of the morning chorus.

"Everyone move port side," orders Nelson, steering hard left to avoid Dingy Skipper, exclaiming, "Wow, that was close!"

Bullfrog, Carrie, runs Riverbanks port, in charge of a motley crew of frog and toad dockers, lifting and lowering goods, then processing and storing for onward transportation or drawing down when needed. Like today, when Catty from Caterpillar Caterers picks up several boxes of peas for delivering to Queen Fishnette. The frog and toad dockers ribbit while they work, each singing a different word from the morning chorus while Carrie bellows every line, her voice croaking under strain, appearing to belch every word.

"Where do we put these carrot sticks, Boss?" enquires frog foreman, Frankie, nibbling a sample from a box dangling from the crane.

"Put them by the apple slices," replies Carrie, pointing to an area for immediate collection. "Caterpillar Caterers will pick them up later in time for school lunches!"

Crickets, Buddy and Hollie, are hanging out at Lorna's Diner with fellow *Leftside Rockers*, all dressed in identical black leather jackets, hair greased and quiffed.

"Grass-shakes all round, please, Lorna," orders Buddy, everyone sat on toadstools.

"Grath-thakes, coming right up!" lisps Lorna, the grass snake, serving her notorious green grass-shakes, sipped and sucked through long blades of grass.

The crickets slurp, chirp and jive to the morning chorus, twisting hips and rocking legs, and providing orchestral percussion with sounds of maracas and tambourines. The corner jukebox blasts out its heavy drumbeat in time to Buddy and Hollie's dance routine of *three steps forward, shake, three steps back, shake, turning to the right then repeating.*

On a small clearing next to the diner, Mo, the grasshopper conducts martial arts for his *early bird* class. A dozen or so grasshoppers face Mo in his black karategi outfit and mimic every move with a sense of serenity and composure. In slow motion, they fist-punch the air with one arm after another then leg-chop and karate kick fresh air, ending every morning chorus line with a single chant before pivoting and coming to a standstill with a bow and praying hands.

"Hei," the grasshoppers chant, hearing *As the dawn sunrises,* changing moves to *Seeking, coaxing, catching prizes,* chanting once more, "Hei!"

Mo then takes them through a series of breathing exercises and meditation to flush away any stresses and to prepare for the challenges ahead.

Millipede, Millie, offers to treat her children to a grass-shake on account of it being baby Billie's birthday. "Get your boots on," she shouts, tapping her feet to the morning chorus and making quite a racket. "We must hurry!"

"Can you help us?" the children plead, looking in trepidation at the vast boot rack, further impeded by Millie's running shoes, unceremoniously cast-off after a midnight jog.

"Sure," replies Millie, helping to put on their boots, forgetting and underestimating how long it takes!

Wood pigeon timber merchants, Travis and Purrkins, are busy cutting and carrying a variety of wood and insulation materials for tradesfolk completing essential repairs around and about.

Hedgehog builder, Harry, checks his list. "I'd like two, two by twos, four, four by fours, and three, three by..."

"Don't tell me," anticipates Travis, magically pulling a pencil from behind his ear, "three, three by threes."

"No," replies Harry, rechecking his list. "Three, three by twos!"

"Any nails?" enquires Purrkins, operating the cash till.

"I'm good for nails!" replies Harry, displaying his spines like a sewer's pincushion. "As you can see, I have an endless supply!"

Cabinet maker and part-time sculptor, woodpecker, Rodin, is very fussy when it comes to choosing wood, notorious for picking holes in any timber on offer. Consequently, Travis and Purrkins like to pull his leg, teasing, "How much wood would a woodpecker pick if a woodpecker could pick wood?"

"He would pick, he would, as much as he could," replies Rodin, retrieving a fob watch from his smock pocket, unaware that they are jerking his chain as he examines the notches in a single piece of pine, adding, "and pick as much wood as a woodpecker would if a woodpecker could pick wood!"

A platoon of soldier ants stretcher wounded ants and insects, knocked over and stepped on the day before. While serjeant Hill commands his troops to head for Silk House Surgery, the caring nurse ants tend to and hold the hands of the injured. Hearing the morning chorus rallies spirits, injecting hope as bystanders line the path to wave multi-coloured flags and applaud, banging anything to hand.

The procession passes *The Honey Trap*, a market stall run by bumblebees, Mumble and Stutter, selling beeswax candles, honeycomb sweets and various flavoured honey drinks on tap, ranging from floral lavender and orchard apple to dark liquorice and fruity gooseberry. Mumble pours while Stutter flies back and forth, offering refreshments. Even serjeant Hill gulps down a mug of honey and lemon, soothing his throat before barking marching orders.

"Let's pick up the pace," serjeant Hill bawls, thrusting his baton beneath his armpit. "We can't keep the doctor at bay."

Arriving at the Silk House Surgery, Doctor Ida, the spider rushes out, carrying several black leather bags. She spins her silk bandages around the broken limbs, supported with twigs, tackling two at a time with her eight flailing legs, wrapping and binding like a possessed pianist playing chords and rippling keys. Head nurse ant, Antonia assists until the last one is finished then serjeant Hill marches the patched-up troop back to the nest for recuperation, in time to the morning chorus.

Eartha, the worm, disguises as a member of Caterpillar Caterers, modifying her walk with superimposed feet, face painting green and wearing a large chef's hat which she pulls right down. Neither Rob nor Bob recognises her as she wanders past the café, carrying a vatful of snake oil to Silk House Surgery.

"Morning, boys," shouts Eartha, pushing her luck, "Lovely day!"

Late risers, dormouse, Daphne, field mouse, Fred, water vole, Vince, pygmy shrew, Sheila, and brown rats, Rachael and Roland, are yawning and stretching downstream on the right side of the bank where it is less chaotic. They are about to begin their morning swim which they fondly call *the rat race*, adjusting swimming caps and checking that costumes are not going to fail during the initial dive! Rachael and Roland have the advantage of size, and Vince is a born natural while Fred and Daphne are timid but enjoy the daily exercise. Darkhorse, Sheila may be small, but she can hold her breath for long periods, shrewdly swimming underwater like a slithering eel and beating everyone every time.

"On the last line of the morning chorus," dictates Fred, lifting his arm. "On your marks, get set, go!" dropping his arm to *no surprises* as all six swallow-dive, some better than others!

The morning chorus turns from a tune of joy and awakening to one of melancholy and sad lament. Margot, the escargot, leads the funeral procession, scattering white rose petals as she goes. Bullet, the slug, affectionately and ironically nicknamed, pall bears sister, Lettice's coffin, laden with floral tributes on display for all to see.

Bullet is mourning Lettice's untimely death a few days before, finding her lifeless body, squashed outside Lancaster Cottage rear door. Carrying a previous injury, Lettice could not escape the exiting red welly, ending the life of a beautiful mind with exciting ambitions to follow in Margot's slimy footsteps and achieve first homeownership by the end of the year.

Everyone stops to lower heads in respect. Crows, Barton and Barbara, ravens, Beyoncé and Destiny, and single magpie, Sorrow, perch on the brick wall, and squawk and caw a moving funeral march.

Then, just as Margot and Bullet pass Fisher Mongers, the back door to York Cottage flies open and outsteps Primrose in a white dressing gown and white fluffy slippers, clutching a cup of tea and munching a slice of toast.

Riverbanks goes into survival mode, erring on every visitor being a potential foe rather than a friendly face. It is pandemonium to the untrained eye, a well-rehearsed and cohesive drill to all concerned. Following protocols defined by King Fisher and Queen Fishnette, all actions are go!

King Fisher guzzles down the remaining stock, while Prince Fishin extinguishes the barbecue, and Queen Fishnette and Princess Fishelle gather the pea and mint sauces, all flying home on the right bank, hiding from sight, still wearing aprons.

Dylan and Thomas, mouths now closed and breathing through noses, reverse, hover, then skim down Watermill Stream like propelled and bouncing pebbles, quaffing cooling water as they go before exiting through the distant brick arch.

Chav and her friends congregate on nearby telephone wires, echoing the notes of the morning chorus score.

Buddy and Hollie and the Leftside Rockers, hop into the safety of the adjacent long grass, followed by Lorna who pulls down the diner shutters and slinks away to her secret hiding place. Mo and his class, hop, skip and long jump into the shelter of nearby flower beds and bushes, blending into the background, knees trembling in fear.

Jack and Jimmy wheelbarrow their baskets and boxes into Watermill Stream and scarper in separate directions, flying wild around the gardens while Harriet and Hettie head for the security of Riverbanks Hotel. Dunny, Putz, Bozo and Kwim, carry on regardless, showering and towel-drying customers, applying product and aftershave. Clarice says nothing, preserving her voice for later, dashing around the gardens with apparent nonchalance.

Vince, Rachael and Roland swim back home on the right bank while Daphne, Fred and Sheila scuttle up the bank and back to respective homes somewhere in Lancaster garden.

Margot withdraws into her shell while Bullet is typically slow to react, attempting unsuccessfully to break into Margot's home to avoid a similar fate to Lettice.

Frankie, together with the other frog and toad dockers, searches sanctuary amongst the reeds while Carrie camouflages without lifting a finger.

Travis and Purrkins cover the timber with the insulation material to resemble a simple pile of twigs and dried vegetation, and fly off like two clays, endeavouring to avoid buckshot. Harry chucks away his wood and turns into a ball, rolling into the shrubbery like a croqueted ball, driven off-court. Rodin, still to select, flies home empty-handed, knocking loudly in time to the morning chorus, impatient for his housemates to open the door.

Doctor Ida covers Nurse Antonia in silk bandages and carries to safety in the centre of her web, the dew more or less gone as the sun intensifies.

Bryan and the water boatmen hide under their acorn cups. White Admiral Nelson and the other skippers jettison supplies overboard and abandon lily pads, fluttering away in all directions, somehow missing each other in the mayhem.

Eartha goes underground. Catty and the Caterpillar Caterers seek refuge, remaining entirely still and consuming any undelivered contents in their possession.

Millie and the children, dejected and moaning, begin to remove their boots, having just completed this most arduous and thankless task.

Mumble and Stutter cover beeswax candles under petals and discard the honeycomb sweets to the floor for any opportune passer-by, before buzzing this way and that unsteadily, inebriated after downing their unsold nectar.

Lord and Lady Bird escort Gordon and the Scarab Prince and his entourage into protection bestowed by the basement of the bronze statue, while Lennon packs away his music and hides beneath the piano.

Barton and Barbara distract Primrose with a frenetic and sped-up version of the morning chorus. Simultaneously, soul-singing Beyoncé and Destiny fly high into a neighbouring tree to draw Primrose's gaze, and Sorrow glides down to rest upon the sundial, attracting Primrose's attention with fervent clicks to make her scour the garden in search of Sorrow's sister, Joy.

Sam and Ella throw the peapod milk into Watermill Stream to keep cool for later collection. Tyrol and Sam gobble into their cheeks as many nuts as they can then scale the closest tree, leaping onto the brick wall to sprint out of sight. Ella wheelbarrows unused sacks to her dry store – a white ceramic gnome cottage complete with a tall chimney and stable doors.

Rob and Bob close Early Bird's Café, handing their waistcoat and apron to Robyn and Bruna, who fly home with mouths full of unsold merchandise to feed their impatient hungry children.

Acting as a final decoy like tricksters using distraction for deception, Rob flies over to Primrose and lands on her garden table like a long-lost friend while Bob replaces Sorrow on the sundial. Together they sing the morning chorus in full voice, while serjeant Hill and his platoon tidy giveaway remnants and close Watermill Stream market to resume once more tomorrow.

Oblivious, Primrose smiles and throws Rob and Bob each a crumb of toast, just as the garden flowers begin to lift their weary heads and bloom into life for the welcoming sun.

3
Bonfires, beekeeping and muck spreading!

Rosemary, dressed in red dungarees tucked into calf-high red wellies, rolls up the sleeves of her complimentary coloured green linen shirt and adjusts the angle of her straw hat with its red silk band, a tied scarf, ends flowing over at the rear to shoulder length and functioning as a makeshift fly deterrent. She opens the large oak double doors and side entrance to her garden, delicately directing farmer, Stanley Thomas, reversing a trailer of cow muck with his old faithful Fergusson, a rusting red tractor, affectionately referred to as Gussie.

The midday sun cooks the already steaming manure, wafting its nauseous smell like an overripe *stinky bishop*. Rosemary counters the putrid odour by breathing through her mouth in contrast to Primrose, who dives inside, shutting all windows and air-spraying every room, attempting to combat impregnation of her furniture fabrics.

"At least *I* do it earlier in the year," Primrose talks aloud to herself, pretending Rosemary is present, "when it's colder, and when windows are closed."

Primrose spreads this natural fertiliser around her white roses in early spring and again in late autumn. Typically, rivalrous, she opts for pig muck, claiming superior quality. Rosemary, on the contrary, believes it is better to cloak her red roses during the height of summer, and by allowing the well-rotted reconstituted grass to ferment longer improves its potency and enables more efficient transpiration into a thirstier crop.

"It's just because her red roses must recover from the demand," Primrose continues to complain rhetorically, smirking, "of the Valentine's Day massacre!"

Stanley is a deft driver but navigating through such a tight squeeze and to such confusing instruction, challenges both his skill and his patience.

"Right a bit," Rosemary yells over the roar of the chugging engine, immediately correcting to, "left a bit," when Stanley turns the steering wheel right, sending the trailer to the left.

Stanley dumps his load, bids farewell and makes a quick exit, turning left towards arable and dairy, Woodville farm, once a tenanted farm of Woodville Castle, now owned by Stanley, his three sons and four daughters. Past generations farmed wheat, milled into flour at Watermill, presently sent to modern facilities handling larger volumes and extracting more from superior spikes. Once catering to the surrounding area, the daily milk also disappears into the national food chain, unlikely to occupy local supermarket shelves, now sold in generic and anonymous packaging.

Local farmers' markets are resurrecting traditional practises, encouraging locally sourced produce and promoting a strong sense of community. However, uncompetitive premiums require significant shifts in consumer habits, realistically long term rather than representing a recent fad.

Wearing red and green suede gloves, Rosemary wheelbarrows the dwindling pyramid to all areas of her garden, pitchforking and trowelling the dark nutritional spread while pruning deadheads and singing words of encouragement. A simple lyric passed down the Lancaster family tree, and she swears the icing on the cake to her prize-winning success. Without set music, Rosemary improvises or adapts a familiar tune or melody, often running out of luck with the rhyming, working out that the famous *Happy birthday* works as good as any.

Red roses, are you ready?
On your marks, get set and go
Rich and vivid, so ruddy
Now is the right time to grow!

Kneeling on her foam cushion like a praying churchgoer, Rosemary pulls down her red and blue bandana, placed initially over nose and mouth to dilute the stench. Now accustomed, she transforms from a Mexican bandit to a country bumpkin, the knotted handkerchief wrapping loosely around her neck, allowing her face to breathe and for the sweat to evaporate. Rosemary cups each rose like a sommelier discerning the attributes and vintage of fine wine. The rose fragrant perfume transcends all. Meanwhile, bees do-si-do from one flower to another, gorging on nectar, inadvertently covering with pollen in return. An essential unwritten contract instinctively understood and religiously honoured, dating back to the invention of honey.

A robin follows Rosemary's every move, rushing to check for titbits whenever she steps back. Rosemary convinces herself that the robin understands when he moves his head side to side. "What a lovely day it is again, Rudy," Rosemary says, unknowingly pet-naming *him* differently to Primrose who calls *her* Marion after Robin Hood. "Sorry about the smell, although somehow, something tells me that you don't mind."

•

Primrose finally musters the courage to exit York Cottage late afternoon. She is wearing a white laboratory coat over stonewash blue jeans and calf-high white wellies and is sporting a handmade mask, sewn moments before using remnants of fine cornflowers printed on white cotton.

Carrying a clipboard, Primrose heads for her potting shed of substantial brick and glass construction extending from the left boundary wall. It is here that science and nature combine, forever in search of the perfect white rose, a fuller bloom, larger petals, more fragrance, longer stamen and uniform pitching of shark tooth-like thorns. Primrose tends to her succulents, scribbling notes and ticking boxes on her clipboard like a register-taking teacher, instead referring to samples by number rather than by name. This honour only bestowed when chosen to compete or to sell.

Primrose, unlike Rosemary, refuses to adopt artificial chemicals, seeking natural solutions, such as changing the acidity of the soil with various fruit and foliage or varying the quantity and quality of the water source. Purity is the name of her game while Rosemary, in her identical mirror image potting shed, experiments with various human-made fertilisers, genetic mutations and lengthy exposure to the elements including twenty-four-seven artificial sunlight. In the quest to create the most seductive red and heart-shaped silhouette, taking inspiration from some Grimm story or stretching back to the Genesis of time and naively doing the devil's work.

Untrusting of each other, Primrose padlocks her potting shed and heads inside to prepare dinner. Rosemary, muck-marked from head to toe, sits on her decking and sips tea from her gloss red cup and saucer, admiring a job well done.

Primrose steps back outside to enjoy a well-earned cup of tea on her decking, sipping from a white china cup and saucer, but forgetting her mask. The smell nose punches Primrose, forcing recollection of some forsaken festival and an unfortunate lack of facilities.

"What a pong, Rosemary?" Primrose complains loudly over the fence, putting on a brave face and resting her cup and saucer close to her face.

"It's a mucky job," jests Rosemary, laughing at her own joke, "but someone has to do it!"

Primrose overlooks the blatant pun and laughs back just as the sprinklers in both gardens erupt into life, showering everything like a Sun King vista of Versailles. The refracting sunlight reflects in every droplet and projects zoetrope rainbows of various size and intensity like a candy clad paradise. There is nothing for either to say but look and admire.

•

With summer drawing to an end, inviting autumn to fall, there are marked changes for those who bother to observe. The sunlight has a translucency, glowing rather than shining. The air feels lighter and fresher, aided by subtle drops in temperature. Sounds ring another way, noticeably hollower, echoing longer. The morning exaggerates these variances like a musical genius interpreting identical notes, playing neither better nor worse, but stirring different emotions within the listener. Regardless, the morning begins again like every other fine morning, with

Primrose existing York Cottage to a warm welcoming from Marion and blackbird, Martin, pet-named after the King of civil rights. Except, today, Primrose swaps her dressing gown and toast for white beekeeping overalls, a wide-brimmed white hat with encircling black veil, white wellies, and holds a long-nosed smoker in white suede elbow-length gloves like some alien has landed.

Rosemary, in her own words, requires more *beauty sleep*, an excuse she perpetuates to disguise a propensity for burning the midnight oil and a love affair with her four-poster and its plush pillows and hugging mattress. She struggles to surface much before nine, opening her florist mid-morning, content to sacrifice the early-bird orders, confident that customers will accommodate and call when the time is right.

Primrose considers early morning and sunrise in particular, dependent on the time of year, to be the most inspiring part of the day when distraction still dreams and when the brain is at its most alert and efficient, recharged like an overused mobile phone. She enjoyed opening her florist early but found that the majority favoured a Rosemary work ethic, ordering or purchasing flowers later in the day. Subsequently, early morning is best spent tending to and harvesting her white roses, an exclusive and much sought-after supply, far superior to the cheaper strain she stocks to satisfy the tighter purse.

Primrose recognises that the health and constant rejuvenation of her flowers relies on the well-being and strength of the resident bees. Consequently, she manages a single hive, in exchange for collecting the delectable tasting honey at the end of each summer. She decants the God-given golden gloop into exquisite pentagonal glass jars, and labels with her white rose emblem and York Cottage title, simply calling *honey from heaven*. Primrose is more than aware that the bees collect nectar from both gardens, but rationalises that Rosemary is too lazy and could do the same, instead, choosing not to. Primrose claims, "Her loss is my gain."

Rosemary says, "She's welcome to the sticky stuff!" retaliating, "Who would want to wear one of those ridiculous outfits and hang about with so many things that sting!"

Resembling an emergency worker in isolation and avoiding contamination, Primrose ignites the smoker, pumping the bellows until it exhales smoke like a behind the bike shed teenager. Holding her honey frame carrier in one hand and the smoker in the other, she wanders slowly to the far-left corner of the garden, home to an impressive hive housing several supers.

Primrose observes a family of kingfishers, flying expertly up and downstream, and a group of tits washing and preening their feathers in the birdbath, preparing for the day ahead. Sidestepping a slug and a snail, she takes care to avoid a trail of ants, and not to disturb freshly spun spiderwebs, their creators lying dormant, dead centre, an occasional victim, gagged and bound, held captive.

Primrose approaches the beehive, its modernist architecture paying homage to minimalism with a hint of flatpack furniture, standing tall as a simple white tower and an honest flat roof. Albeit with no Allen bolts, just a hexagonal single entrance and exit. An outdoor clock on the garden brick wall displays the time. The white roses do their best to assist, blooms beaming, casting *come and get me* spell-like pheromones.

Preferring to harvest hive by hive and three honey supers at a time, Primrose faces several days to complete. She is banking on the female workers being hungry and eager to vacate with a sting in their tails, in search of the final nectar, leaving behind the impotent drones - males more interested in servicing the queen than protecting the hive.

"I bet a few Rosemarys are lurking behind," thinks Primrose, careful to maintain silence, mocking, "oversleeping and leaving things to the last minute!" as she hides the hive in a cloud of calming smoke, taking no chances, unstacking and cutting the hive in half.

Bees swarm roundabout. A handful of workers attempt to attack through the impenetrable suit, wasting ammunition on this friendly foe. With an extra puff of smoke, Primrose retrieves a wax-capped honey frame, encouraging stubborn drones to depart, to relocate into the new structure, to begin redecorating all over again. Primrose spots the queen, dominant and grander, holding court, reluctant to vacate. "Come on queenie," whispers Primrose, studying every move with fascination before adding, empathetically, "I know moving home is stressful and one of the biggest challenges in life, but it always works out for the best. It's not as if I am evicting you out onto the street, making you homeless or vagrant.

"You have more room to house all those lovely children," Primrose continues like a well-rehearsed sales agent. "I'm adding another level at the top of the house where they can stay and give you some peace and quiet!"

Primrose rebuilds the hive and returns home to begin the process of extraction, turning honey into money. Before leaving, a group of mischievous and disobedient ducklings swim through the brick arch, excitedly quacking as if entering Santa's grotto then quacking dejectedly in response to a mother duck and father drake recalling them from the other side. Primrose smiles at the thought of nature mirroring humankind, remembering this certainty given mammalian status.

•

Late afternoon sees Rosemary return from the florist to check on her succulents and ongoing experiments. She leaves the door to the potting shed ajar, unintentionally as she heads to the far end of the garden, rake in hand, to finish building a bonfire.

Rosemary passes the red apple tree, groaning under the weight of perfectly ripe fruit. She picks a low hanging apple, biting into its protective skin, and releasing a flurry of apple juice to dribble down her chin, forcing a backhanded swipe. Savouring the distinctive taste and consistency of her apple, Rosemary attempts to estimate the crop, dividing into jars of chutney, apple pies and cartons of freshly squeezed juice.

Something catches her eye.

A wasp nest hangs towards the top of the apple tree, dangling like a large paper lantern, vibrating with a low buzz and a haze of bright yellow and black. "Clever things," she exclaims, shaking her head at the prospect of owning such an unexploded bomb, altering the phrase, "If the fruit will not come to Muhammad, then Muhammad must go to the fruit!"

Resigned to a more challenging apple harvest, Rosemary continues raking the final vegetation. Standing back to marvel, she curtsies before her bonfire, lighting a match and setting alight the pile of easy-to-burn kindle. Stereotypically, the ensuing smoke follows Rosemary like annoying flies to a long-suffering cow, causing her to cough and splutter and cry soothing tears to alleviate stinging eyes. The distinct sound of a distant woodpecker distracts her gaze as she looks to locate its exact position before the drilling ends as quickly as it begins. Then something rustles in the rosebushes behind, but there is no time to investigate.

"Watch that doesn't go berserk, Rosemary," Primrose shouts from across the stream while retrieving more honey frames. "You know what happened last time."

"Yes, Yes," replies Rosemary, indignantly, never happy with criticism, especially from busy-body Primrose. "It's all under control, Primrose," she says through gritted teeth, kicking one side of the bonfire with her red welly.

Post pruning, the last bonfire grew into the perfect storm, too large for the surroundings and with traces of flammable fertiliser, sending a fireball twenty feet high to threaten the apple tree, scorching the skins of the proximate like sunbathers asleep during the midday sun. After a dozen red buckets of stream water, the bonfire lay drenched and impossible to relight.

Rosemary glances at the red bucket, conveniently stowed in the far corner, praying that it remains, especially in front of a gloating Primrose. This year's bonfire is smokier than usual, doused by a light summer shower the day before. The smoke engulfs the apple tree, snaking its way through the maze of branches and fruit until it reaches the wasp nest. Perturbed as any homeowner would be to find smoke seeping through every hallway and into every room, the fearful inhabitants make a hasty escape, teeming in anger. Already notorious for being both clumsy and bad-tempered during late summer, gate-crashing every picnic and crash-landing every sugary drink, the smoke effect is tenfold, forcing uncontrollable *vespas* to scoot this way and that and to attack everything in sight.

Rosemary places the bonfire between her and the manic traffic, witnessing a handful of late-working bees fall victim to unwarranted hate crimes. Like a territorial gang stamping authority on straying opponents, the yellow-jacket perpetrators see red and beat into submission unsuspecting bystanders with no regard for the consequences or the health of the injured parties.

The diminishing smoke, fuelled by the heat of the intensifying bonfire, has a calming effect. The wasp nest becomes a place of sanctuary once more, summoning back its unremorseful, happy to abandon unwitting targets.

Wetting the cinders to coincide with the failing light, Rosemary retires to the comfort of home. Before padlocking the potting shed, she ejects a pair of desperate bumblebees - exhausted and padding every surface in search of an exit, not smart enough to retrace their steps. The bumblebees fly away like aeroplanes with engine trouble, emergency landing by the stream, desperately seeking water.

Rosemary detects the smell of smoke on her clothes as she approaches the back door, remarking with a hint of annoyance, "I only washed these yesterday."

4
Forest fires, earthquakes and landslides!

"I didn't see you at the market this morning, Bullet," says Margot, carrying a box of rotten vegetables, sold for next to nothing by Caterpillar Caterers at the end of each market, always provoking a rush.

"I'm feeling a little sluggish," jokes Bullet, putting on a brave face, resting beneath a red rose bush. "Getting up seems so much harder these days."

"It'll take time, Bullet," consoles Margot, offering a piece of blackened carrot on the verge of turning to mulch. "It's only been a few weeks since Lettice left this wonderful world. Time is a great healer, especially when we miss the ones we love."

"I'm trying, Margot," replies Bullet, desolately, unable to look her in the face, "but everywhere I look, something reminds me of Lettice."

Bullet points to an array of dried slime trails, heading in different directions, sometimes crisscrossing, shimmering in the morning light. "I'm afraid that once these have gone, she will fade forever, and become a forgotten memory," he agonises.

"Nonsense, Bullet," dismisses Margot, sharing his pain. "She will always be in our memory, forever and ever." Margot hands her box of goodies to Bullet. "Here. Take this and spend some time building your strength."

"I couldn't, Margot," says Bullet, attempting to return the box. "I know how much demand there is for these leftovers. Almost a daily riot."

"You need to look after yourself, Bullet, and let grief take its course," insists Margot, holding her hands to her chest, smiling. "It will be my pleasure to fetch your food until you're as right as rain."

"That's very kind, Margot," thanks Bullet, happy to have someone care. "I will never forget this, I promise."

A dark cloud appears, forcing Margot and Bullet to look up. Engrossed in conversation, they miss the arrival of *Red Wellies*, a giant that dominates and spreads fear over the right-hand garden of Watermill Stream. Unable to react or escape, a forkful of cow muck falls from above, covering them both like losing contestants in an entertaining quiz show. With Margot managing to find safety in her shell, and Bullet shrinking his build half-size, the pair avoids subsequent blows to spread the pungent poultice evenly.

Like a surfacing diver, Bullet raises his head above the parapet, checking that the coast is clear then looking in vain for Margot. "Margooohhh!" shouts Bullet, splashing about, imagining the worst. "As if life couldn't get any worse," he exclaims, searching the surrounding sea of muck.

Margot pops out her head, pulling up to float upon the surface.

"Thank goodness," exclaims Bullet, hugging Margot, "I thought I'd lost you, too."

"Look around, Bullet," instructs Margot, sinking into the muck and wallowing in delight, "It's heaven. As if someone or something from above heard our anxiety and showered us with paradise!"

Bullet inhales deeply, exhaling in ecstasy as the smell smacks the back of his throat, reflexes rolling his eyes back to front in elation.

"No need to queue for leftovers, Margot," says Bullet, roly-polying the mountain of muck. "This will last forever."

"Life's funny sometimes," philosophises Margot, submerging her head into the manure like a Halloween apple bobber, "it can be cruel but also kind."

"Nevermind that," responds Bullet, climbing to the top once more. "Lettice would find this so funny. To see me as happy as a pig in muck!"

"Yes, she would," acknowledges Margot, attempting to roly-poly unsuccessfully, then sniffing the aroma like a cordon blue chef, joking, "to see you as happy as a cow in muck!"

"Watch and learn, children," brags King Fisher, standing on one side of Watermill Stream and Queen Fishnette on the other, videoing for prosperity. "Watch and learn."

"We've seen this a thousand times," remarks Prince Fishin, tutting and rolling his eyes at Princess Fishelle. "You stand perfectly still and cast your rod into deep water, ideally where changes in colour or darkening of shadows occur."

"Then wait patiently for the fish to take the bait," adds Princess Fishelle, trying to inject enthusiasm into her voice. "or repeatedly cast your rod, mimicking a fly or an insect, tricking the fish to the surface to sink their chops into the barbed hook hidden within."

"If you have the know-how, clever-clogs," interjects Queen Fishnette, pausing the camera, "then why can't you do it?"

"Because it's so boring," moans Prince Fishin, pulling out his phone to respond to a friend's post, pressing *like* and tippy tapping a reply.

"And barbaric," declares Princess Fishelle, revealing her save-the-fish T-shirt. "What have fish ever done to us?"

"My father taught me how to fish," explains King Fisher, repeating a story he has told many times, "his father taught him and his..."

"...father taught him, and so on and so on, back to when the Fishers were working-class and farming bluebottle maggots for a living!" finishes Prince Fishin, seeing the dejection in his father's face as King Fisher packs away the equipment.

Suddenly, Queen Fishnette raises the alarm, using the official colour code assigned to the respective garden giants who periodically visit, who transform or bring mayhem to Riverbanks.

"White Wellies!" she shouts, thrusting her camera into her handbag and flying over to join the others.

"They're coming this way," alerts King Fisher, chucking the fishing tackle and keep nets over his shoulder, and grabbing the rods. "Meet you all by the brick arch."

King Fisher and his family fly downstream, Prince Fishin returning momentarily to pick up his mobile phone, dropped accidentally and smashing the screen yet again.

•

The stirring crescendo of Puccini's Nessun Dorma bellows from The Barber Quartet. Dunny, Putz, Bozo and Kwim reminisce previous football world cups, raising and lowering their barber chairs in time to the score, almost launching their customers to the heavens for the finale. All four barbers bow to the enthusiastic applause before resuming normal play.

"Are you going to the match at the weekend, Putz?" asks Dunny, wiping away the tears with his white handkerchief. "Should be a good game."

"Riverpool versus Chaffield United," nods Putz, spraying potent aftershave onto customer Barton's face. "The Tits versus The Chaff. Always a close fought match."

"The reds versus the whites," expands Dunny, afro-combing customer Bob's hair, he and Putz chanting, "C'mon you reds."

"The winner plays my team, Chelstream. The Blue Tits," informs Bozo, massaging customer Rob's head with conditioner. "Wouldn't it be great if it was an all tit final?" dreams Bozo, carried away and pressing too hard into Rob's temples, teasing Dunny and Putz. "Chelstream thrashing Riverpool four one in extra-time."

"It'll be my team next year," adds Kwim, clipping Sorrow's hair with a *number one* short back and sides. "Second division, Yellow Tits."

"Remind me of your team again, Kwim," asks Dunny, in-joking with Putz and Bozo.

"Whatford," Kwim announces proudly, mispronouncing as What for, holding the hand mirror to show Sorrow the back of his head.

"So, we know which team you support!" punchline delivers Dunny, causing Putz and Bozo to titter.

"Very funny, I'll give you *what for!*" strikes Kwim as Sorrow mourns his severe hair loss and insists, he requested a *number four*.

All four customers complete simultaneously, admiring themselves in the mirror, pulling faces and posing heads, imagining the lucky recipient swooning over their new look.

"Happy, Barton?" enquires Putz, removing the gown and brushing away prevalent dandruff.

"I'm getting old, Putz!" replies Barton, stroking his smooth chin while examining his crow's feet, and smelling like a department store ground floor.

"Laughter lines," compliments Putz, adding, "revealing life's storylines and hiding nothing between the lines."

"Nobody can cut hair like yours, better than me, Bob!" self-congratulates Dunny, confidently nodding and combing over his side parting while brushing unwanted hair to the floor.

"I salute you, Dunny," praises Bob, tongue in cheek, astounded by Dunny's ego as a great tit and not a blackbird, further mocking, "and I would kneel before you if I weren't already sitting down."

"Thank you, Bob," responds Dunny, oblivious, tweeting his latest success under the banner *making great hair again*.

"What do you think of your new haircut, Rob?" asks Bozo, roughing his own hair for mutual effect. "Wild's the new smart."

"I wanted something more conservative," replies Rob, trying in vain to flatten his new unruly mop top. "I don't want to labour the point, but I want the old smart if this is the new smart."

"No problem, Rob," says Bozo, reaching for the hairdryer, "I'm more than happy to go with the flow...change with the wind... make a U-turn down a blind alley...revisit the negotiating table again and again. It's no problem at all."

"I'm not sorry, Sorrow," declares Kwim, throwing fuel on the fire, "You asked for a number one, and I gave you a number one."

"You need to test your ears," retaliates Sorrow with a face of thunder. "You've dropped a real bombshell, Kwim and made me look like a right fool."

"I think you look distinctive," replies Kwim, conceding some, realising how powerful is Sorrow. "You are unique. There's no one quite like you."

As Barton, Bob, Rob and Sorrow leave The Barber Quartet to continue their day, Barton with a bird's eye view of the garden spies the familiar white giant. Even more monstrous and out-of-this-world, wearing sinister white armour and hiding behind a deathly veil, cloaked in a cloud of smoke.

"White Wellies!" he shouts back to alert The Barber Quartet, fading into the distance as he flies off to scare farmers attending their crops. "Coming straight for you. Coming to expel you with gaaasss..."

Dunny, Putz, Bozo and Kwim only hear *White Wellies!* Reluctant to vacate the shop in such a mess, they carry on sweeping and preparing for the next customers, ready to chance their arms against an apparent enemy who only seems to assist business, supplying fresh water and snacks whenever needed.

•

Bullet is assisting Margot to move home in gratitude for helping him get over his sister's untimely death. Only moving across the road rather than to the other side of the garden, they decide not to engage professionals and relay her stuff in boxes, allocating a full day given their combined speed of next to nothing.

"You seem so much happier, Bullet," suggests Margot, carrying one end of a dining table and edging backwards, stopping every few steps to adjust her grip.

"I am, Margot, thanks to you and good old father time," Bullet says with a smile. "The turning point was the day the heavens opened and covered us in muck."

"That was one of the best days of the year," remembers Margot, asking Bullet to swap ends. "They don't come much better."

"And your idea for a memorial bench along Watermill Stream where Lettice and I played as kids," continues Bullet, taking forever to change ends and to find a suitable grip, "has given me a place to go when I'm feeling down. To remember the good times, even when we argued or got on each other's nerves."

A distant rumble becomes louder and louder. The ground quivers underfoot then trembles as the familiar pattern unfolds.

"White Wellies!" exclaims Margot, catching sight of the approaching shiny rubber boots with unforgiving soles ready to grind the unfortunate into the ground and inside their deep-rutted grips.

Margot and Bullet dive under the dining table as the earthquakes, swaying them side to side, threatening to open up and swallow them whole.

"I'm too young to die!" screams Bullet, holding onto Margot as if his life depended. "I don't want to go the same way as Lettice."

"Be brave, Bullet," urges Margot, fearing too for her life, praying with closed eyes as White Wellies, unbeknown, sidesteps at the last moment, thankfully sparing them to live another day and to continue the laborious task of moving home.

•

Crowds of placard bearing anti-establishment ants are congregating on the main boulevard of York Cottage garden that runs parallel to Watermill Stream. A group of yellow meadow ants arrive by lily pad into Riverbanks jetty, wearing their distinctive high-vis jackets. They are demonstrating against the dominance and supremacy of the White Wellies on one side and the Red Wellies on the other that cause disharmony and oppression to their communities, threatening the environment with pollution and unbalancing the natural ecosystem.

A hoard of discontent carpenter ants is protesting against factory owners, Twitt, Twatt and Twott. Three conniving cockroaches, identical except one with jumbo ears, one with a considerable conk and one with no chin, chinless, that duped the carpenters into signing an agreement to dismantle their rights overnight.

Marching mining ants are demanding better working conditions, and demonstrating against the threat of imminent closures, remonstrating the cheaper produce coming into Riverbanks port from further downstream, flooding the market and jeopardising livelihoods.

Bryan and the water boatmen ferry a small group of redwood ants across Watermill Stream. Attending any march where there is a chance for disruption and tipping of the status quo, they wear masks and balaclavas to avoid face recognition despite standing out like a fly in hot soup.

Student ants hitch a lift from Lorna, on her way to open the diner. Dissatisfied with rising tuition fees and the unsatisfactory level of teacher input, they are eager to voice ill-feeling and disregard for social hierarchy as both visionary and revolutionary in equal measures. Unsurprising, many students miss the start, choosing to join mid-flow, unable to stir at such an ungodly hour or leaving banner making to the last minute.

Uncharacteristically, Nurse Antonia and colleagues are complaining about lack of funding and unfair pay, claiming compromises in the delivery of outstanding health care and life-saving procedures at the point of contact. Scores of regular workers are marching in solidarity, wholly in favour and supportive of the apparent injustices consuming Watermill, dreaming of a fairer world and a brighter future for generations to come.

March organisers and newlyweds, Lenin and Luther, are at the helm in high-viz vests and carrying megaphones, repeating the anti-establishment message to ripple along the line like a Mexican wave.

Ants, ants, ants
Anti-this, anti-that, anti-all

The march begins at the sundial to meander peacefully through Riverbanks and to conclude with an ant blockade around the port, hoping to enrol sympathetic frog marchers alongside.

Barely five minutes of progress, when there is a frantic cry of *White Wellies* from the rear. Bedlam ensues as Nurse Antonia and colleagues flee in fear of their lives, discarding placards and screaming hysterically. The Carpenters use their placards to create a *testudo* tortoise formation like a roman legion shielding from an overhead attack. The miners begin burrowing as if burying their heads in the sand will be an adequate defence. The yellow meadows join forces with the redwoods and the common gardens, using anything in reach as missiles, directing at the rapidly approaching white tyrant, hoping to disarm, united in the common belief that yellow, red and black ant lives matter, reinforcing the reasons for marching.

A white welly hovers overhead as if aiming, somewhat indecisively then planting into an open space, incredibly avoiding everyone except Lenin and Luther. Temporarily trampled underfoot between the deeply rutted grip, they emerge unscathed and still chanting through megaphones while White Wellies carries on along the path.

Ants, ants, ants
Anti-this, anti-that, anti-all

•

Further downstream is an ornamental pseudo-stone windmill, gathering moss and lichen. Used only for decoration purposes, it is the perfect front, and the secret location of S.P.I.N - an acronym for Spyder Protocols and Intelligence Network. S.P.I.N is a covert organisation for the protection of Watermill gardens against, terrorism, espionage and sabotage.

Access to the windmill is through a rear manufacturing default, a small hole invisible to the unobservant, leading to an underground cavern and a network of tunnels reaching as far as the brick boundary and boring deep beneath Watermill Stream.

Mole, Freckles is the big wig, handling all internal affairs and computer surveillance, relying on an elite squad of secret agent spiders, known as Spyders, for surface to surface external missions.

"Good morning," welcomes Freckles, disguising with dark glasses to hide her disfigurement, blinded during a failed assignment many years ago. "You are probably wondering why I have called you all here this morning, some of you travelling from remote parts of the gardens and at such short notice. I am delighted that the new S.P.I.N web protocols for communication are working."

Freckles sits behind a large desk, giving an appearance of surveilling the room and looking at each squad member individually, her sense of smell tasked with identifying every odour and idiosyncrasy.

"As you know, there are eight arms to S.P.I.N, each represented by a secret agent Spyder," details Freckles, illuminating an illustrated slide of the S.P.I.N black spider logo and eight abbreviated codes denoting each secret agent attendee. "None of you has met and so today is about bringing you together for special forces and counterintelligence training."

Freckles extends her telescopic pointer to the first arm on the slide, prompting, "Every Spyder, please identify by your secret agent code and introduce the arm you represent, starting with G8."

[Given that eight is lucky and the perfect number of arachnid arms and legs, secret agent codes adopt the number eight text-speak, pronounced *ate*, prefixed with an identifying letter – G8, *Gate* for example.]

"G8, responsible for opening doors and gaining access," begins a geeky and bespectacled Spyder, tapping into the central computer system from his laptop and changing the S.P.I.N logo slide temporarily to a picture of Freckles in a bikini. This flippant action sparks laughter, helping to put everyone at ease. "I'm your agent for anything to do with computers and the worldwide web."

Freckles cannot see the joke, avoiding her embarrassment, and calls for order.

"B8, responsible for setting traps and decoys," follows another bespectacled Spyder, accept athletic and super fit and wearing a utility belt. "Distraction's the name, and entrapment's the aim of the game," continues B8, triggering a series of mini-explosions before throwing silk spun net over Freckles. "I'm your agent for anything to do with gadgets and gizmos."

"I think you've made your point, B8," says Freckles, trying in vain to escape. "Now get this thing off me immediately."

"F8, responsible for monitoring and surveillance," introduces a Spyder taking selfies, covertly recording and listening on a hidden earpiece. "Searching for things out of the ordinary that might affect our future," continues F8, playing back a revealing recording of Freckles asking Doctor Ida for spot cream. "I'm your agent for anything to do with evidence gathering."

"That's quite enough, F8," responds Freckles, placing a hand over her chin to hide an angry boil. "My acne is of no concern to you nor anyone else for that matter."

"L8, responsible for nocturnal affairs," reveals an insipid and pale-skinned Spyder, yawning and stretching. "Think of me while you're tucked up in bed, dreaming and catching up on beauty sleep, except for Freckles it seems..."

"Excuse me, L8," interrupts Freckles, unhappy with the intimation. "Bullying in the workplace is unacceptable."

"If you had let me finish," defends F8, at risk of digging a deeper ditch, "I was going to say, except for Freckles who absolutely doesn't need it!" hoping to have redeemed an awkward situation. "I'm your agent for anything in the dark."

"D8, responsible for planning," outlines a smartly dressed Spyder, wearing several watches displaying different time zones. "Coordinating everything down to the last detail," scanning the calendar on a computer tablet to inform Freckles that Doctor Ida has confirmed an appointment to lance her boil. "I'm your agent for anything to do with logistics."

"Yes, Yes, D8," dismisses Freckles, holding a finger over her mouth to demand discretion, "just send me a calendar invite to accept."

"R8, responsible for assessing risk," says a hard hat-wearing Spyder, ticking boxes on a clipboard. "Ensuring no one comes to any harm, evaluating danger and potential threats," informing Freckles that bringing all agents into one location is an accident waiting to happen. "I'm your agent for anything to do with health and safety."

"Unless there's a mole in the room, R8," responds Freckles, realising her faux pas, "then it's a risk worth taking."

"H8, responsible for defence," bellows a huge Spyder in a low voice with arms and legs the size of punch bags, body bulging over the seat about to break under strain. "Better described as *attack*, dealing with trouble-makers and providing backup," asking Freckles if she wants help sorting out Doctor Ida. "I'm your agent for anything requiring brute force."

"No, H8, absolutely not," condemns Freckles, shifting uncomfortably in her chair, "Doctor Ida's trying to help not hinder."

"M8, last but not least, responsible for public relations," effuses the final Spyder in a smooth, charming voice, dressed immaculately and oozing charisma. "Personally engaging the enemy and using whatever means necessary to extract information," complimenting Freckles on how good she looks in her bikini. "I'm your agent for anything requiring a friendly face."

"That sort of comment is highly inappropriate, M8," scolds Freckles, trying to ascertain how or when M8 saw her in a bikini, "no longer tolerated in today's world of equality and mutual respect."

The Spyders drink tea and converse, some recognising each other from similar parts of the garden. Freckles disappears briefly to reappear alongside an enormous daddy-long-legs. "Can I have your attention, please, Spyders," requests Freckles, looking up at her tremendous, spindly colleague. "This is GR8, our resident tactician and trainer, responsible for taking you through several physical exercises and manoeuvres this morning to improve your abilities and chances of success in the field."

GR8 takes them to an area in Rose Cottage garden away from the windmill, on either side of the meandering path. After a series of aerobic workouts, rope climbing and rope swinging exercises, the Spyders learn different web-spinning techniques to target various prey of differing size and weight. It is not long before silk nets surround the path, some like hammocks, others like undulating blankets, and others more picturesque and hypnotic as floating bull's eyes to capture unsuspecting daydreamers. GR8 shows different coating techniques, rendering some webs almost invisible except under ultraviolet or morning dew. They practice *catch and incapacitate*, taking turns to wrap each other in straight-jackets and dangle like cocoons from rapidly improving weapons otherwise known as webs.

"Code Black Widow!" GR8 shouts like a serjeant major barking orders at inadequate rookies, repeating, "Code Black Widow!"

The Spyders recognise this as the code for White Wellies! Funnel Web is the code for Red Wellies! There is no time to desert, instead opting to lie dead still out of eye-line. One of the webs secures to a branch on the other side of the path. The Spyders watch with anticipation as White Wellies walks through, manoeuvring sideways briefly, but catching the silk thread and jolting F8. Luckily, F8 survives the onslaught to fight another day. GR8 begins again, offering feedback on individual handling of this real-time drill.

•

Queen Abeille, simply referred to as Queen B because she has an annoying habit of spelling out everything, is tended to by valet drones, Spit and Polish, preparing her for another busy day at B Hive. They are brushing her long black hair and manicuring her hands and feet in gold enamel, while she sits in her black silk undergarments awaiting soon-to-arrive new robes.

A moderniser with a disregard for tradition, Queen B has commissioned Lady Bird to design a brand-new beeline. To create a wardrobe fit for a queen, fulfilling the demanding requirements of the modern-day *girl about* B Hive, mixing motherhood with a career and so much more.

It is a simple brief. Smart whilst casual, superior quality whilst easily washable, refined whilst down to earth, projecting personality whilst maintaining practicality, equally at home on the red carpet as on the blue yoga mat, and turning heads, not stomachs. And to include accessories.

"Darling," Queen B says to Buzz, her latest beau and the bee's knees, coincidentally sat beside her, "Be a dear and hand me my mobile phone, spelt P_H_O_N_E."

"Of course, honey," replies Buzz, eager to please and to satisfy her every need. "Where did you put it?"

"It's charging in my office, spelt O_F_F_I_C_E," replies Queen B, gesturing towards the door before scolding. "How many times have I said, not to call me, honey. I am nobody's honey. I am Queen B, Ma'am or your highness, spelt H_I_G_H_N_E_S_S."

"Sorry, hon... I mean Ma'am," corrects Buzz as he exits in search of her phone, Queen B secretly ogling his every saunter.

Buzz is ripped and carrying a six-pack with smouldering good looks and great locks, but while he excels downstairs, unfortunately, Buzz falls short upstairs. He is, however, a great dancer and member of bee band *Pollen Direction*. Queen B fell under his spell, swept off her feet doing the *B Hive Jive* at her recent coronation ball. Rumours of marriage are rife, but Queen B is keeping everything close to her chest, happy to keep her court and courtship at bay. They are the hot couple, the gossip on every bee's lips, papped everywhere they go, the talk of B Hive, Riverbanks and beyond. Inevitably, this union is just another in a very long list for Queen B.

"Hello. Lady Bird. Is that you?" enquires Queen B, dialling a private number.

"Yes. C'est Moi!" replies Lady Bird, affectedly combining languages, unaware with whom she is talking. "Who's this?"

"Queen B," replies Queen B with slight irritation. "I am expecting you, spelt Y_O_U."

"Yes, quite so. Sorry, your highness," says Lady Bird, apologetically. "I am minutes away. Which entrance shall I use?"

"There is only one entrance, spelt E_N_T_R_A_N_C_E, Lady Bird," informs Queen B with excitement. "You can't miss it. My doorbee will escort you to my chambers, spelt C_H_A_M_B_E_R_S."

Queen B ends her call and takes a quick selfie, pouting and crossing her eyes, then posting online with #B4BLINE.

"Lady Bird is on her way up," says Queen B, dismissing Spit and Polish and sending for Princess Wannabee, turning to Buzz once more. "Be a dear and make sure my children are ready for school," she requests, standing in front of the full-size mirror and adding her crown. "They can't keep the birds waiting like yesterday. How can the teacher start without the birds *and* the bees?"

"What is it, mother?" asks Princess Wannabee, waltzing in, wearing a traditional golden gown with horizontal black taffeta and lace banding, and sporting a B Hive hairdo complete with a golden tiara. "I have a dancing lesson soon."

"I have been thinking, spelt T_H_I_N_K_I_N_G," begins Queen B, turning to look her daughter up and down. "What in a bee's world are you wearing, spelt W_E_A_R_I_N_G, Wannabee?"

"None of your beeswax, mother," replies Princess Wannabee, impertinently, deliberately trying to bait Queen B with her over-the-top and provocative dress code.

"We will discuss this later, spelt L_A_T_E_R, Wannabee," responds Queen B, checking the time on her wrist. "I want you to take charge of the workers, spelt W_O_R_K_E_R_S."

"Are you sure, mother?" replies Princess Wannabee, unable to hide her excitement.

"I have received word from production that turnover is down and some of the quality is falling short of our very high standards, spelt S_T_A_N_D_A_R_D_S," details Queen B, gesturing with all thumbs down. "I am entrusting you to remedy this, Wannabee. I suggest taking the workers further afield to the red rose bushes on the other side of Watermill Stream, spelt S_T_R_E_A_M."

"What about Queen V?" questions Princess Wannabee, knowing how territorial their wasp relation can be.

"Our need is greater, Wannabee," replies Queen B, shaking her head, "and cousin Vespula's banter is worse than her sting, spelt S_T_I_N_G."

"You can count on me, mother," reassures Princess Wannabee, delighted with her new status, rolling up her sleeves in preparation.

Princess Wannabee has ideas of her own and eyes on her mother's crown, eager to introduce new protections for the workers and gain greater equality within B Hive. To achieve equal rewards and equal rights, and to promote the dissemination of roles, doing away with stereotypes and encouraging drones and workers to treat each other with mutual respect and dignity. She believes in a modern hive for a changing new world, precariously at risk of eradication and destruction, beyond retrieval if left untouched.

"Super, spelt S_U_P_E_R, Wannabee," says Queen B, pointing to the door. "Now, off you pop. I have Lady Bird arriving any moment, spelt M_O_M_E_N_T."

"Thank you, mother," says Princess Wannabee, smiling from ear to ear, "I won't let you down," teasing, "spelt D_O_W_N!"

Mother and daughter share a giggle as the door opens and in flounces, Lady Bird with her assistant, Lennon in tow, laden with boxes and pushing a wardrobe on wheels, narrowly missing Princess Wannabee on her way out.

"Are you going to make me smile, spelt S_M_I_L_E, Lady Bird?" jests Queen B, clasping her hands like an over-excited child, eager to see her new wardrobe.

"Better than that," replies Lady Bird, requesting Lennon to hand her the first garment, "I will amuse you!"

"Oh, how I like to be amused," nods Queen B, stepping into Lady Bird's beeline clothing and avoiding the mirror until the outfit is complete. "Spelt A_M_U_S_E_D, Lady Bird."

Queen B admires her statement of simplicity, dressed in a black trouser suit made with a wool-silk mixture, the single-breasted jacket open to reveal a simple black and glistening gold striped top. The trousers have a slight flare to accommodate both kitten heels in summer and sturdier boots in winter.

"C'est Elegance with a capital E, your highness." describes Lady Bird, adding a minimal straw bonnet as the final touch, exclaiming, "We are going to bring back the bonnet, Queen B."

Adjusting its angle and nodding, Lady Bird finishes with, "and how better to do that than to have a Queen B in a bonnet."

No sooner does Queen B proclaim, "Bring back the bonnet, spelt B_O_N_N_E_T," than the fire alarm sounds.

Smoke seeps under the door and begins to fill the room. A barrage of noise descends from above, B Hive under attack and disintegrating. Buzz enters, shouting, "We're under attack, your highness. We've got to get you and Lady Bird to safety."

"What about the children," enquires Queen B, switching priorities, "are they safe, spelt S_A_F_E?"

"They left for school five minutes ago," informs Buzz, coughing and spluttering, beginning to lose consciousness.

"Thank goodness," sighs Queen B, despairing, "and Princess Wannabee, is she okay?" unable to spell through worry.

"She left with the workers across Watermill Stream," details Buzz, dead on his feet, unsure how to react.

B Hive moves side to side, quaking down to its foundation as floor after floor crash-lands to earth.

"What are we going to do, Queen B?" Lady Bird asks, attempting to call Lord Bird on her phone but going straight to voicemail.

"I suggest you hide in the wardrobe," replies Queen B, phone calling for reinforcements but finding no signal, "spelt W_A_R_D_R_O_B_E, Lady Bird."

"In you go, Lennon," orders Lady Bird, staring the long nose of adversity in the face. "It's our best chance of survival."

"After you, Lady Bird," says Lennon, loyally and respectfully. "Ladies first."

The ceiling blows away, exposing the sky, turning blue as the smoke subsides. Then the room shoots into the air as if sucked up by a tornado, Queen B and Buzz clinging on for dear life, Lady Bird and Lennon falling to the floor below, wheeling to the edge and toppling overboard, somehow the wardrobe opening and Lady Bird and Lennon jumping to safety.

Queen B grabs a curtain rod as a makeshift spear to joust the anonymous foe, the room shaking more violently and soaring this way and that, colliding with something white and massive, intent on destruction. "Save yourself, Buzz," shouts Queen B, protecting B Hive to the end, declaring, "I love you, spelt I_L_O_V_E_Y_O_U, Buzz."

Buzz throws himself off, unable to hang on any longer, screaming, "I love you, too, honey!" the fresh air lifesaving and carrying him to a nearby rose bush.

"I said, don't call me, honey," Queen B shouts what could be her last words, "spelt H_O_N_E_Y!"

Turning the makeshift spear on herself, Queen B is about to make the ultimate sacrifice, when suddenly the shaking stops and an escape route presents. Queen B grabs her mobile phone and handbag and leaving everything else behind, leaps to the shelter of the open space below.

Inexplicably and exaggerated whenever retold, B Hive miraculously reinstates. Then one by one, migrant workers and deserting drones return home, restoring the community to its former glory, albeit in need of redecoration and tender loving care.

•

Beyond the boundary walls, further downstream where Watermill Stream opens out into a more extensive reservoir before merging with the river, are several teepees and various outdoor sports equipment, home to Shelduck Summer Camp.

"Welcome to your first activity," begin Mallard and Eider, kayak instructors to a handful of young hopefuls, some with previous experience, others novice and attending camp for the first time.

"I'm Mallard," introduces an athletic drake, wearing a white Shelduck T-shirt and brightly coloured swimming shorts, a baseball hat holding sports sunglasses placed backwards for added effect.

"And I'm Eider," adds an equally athletic duck, sporting a red Shelduck T-shirt over a red wetsuit, her baseball hat and sports sunglasses on correctly.

"Hands up, first-timers!" asks Mallard, counting the raised arms, instructing, "You five are with me, the remaining three with Eider."

"Everyone grab a life vest and a paddle and bring your kayaks to the water's edge," directs Eider, detailing, "Mallard will go through some basic skills with the newbies while I share some advanced techniques with the others."

Not long later, after three near-drownings, a broken paddle and one sunken kayak, which incidentally, has never happened before, Mallard believes his group is ready to join Eider's.

"We're going to kayak upstream as far as the brick wall and then back again for some lunch," informs Mallard, smiling at Eider as he arranges everyone in a line. "Everybody ready?"

"Yes, Mallard," answers Eider before anyone else, repeating a much-used joke as if told for the first time. "It looks like our ducks are in a row!"

After much groaning and several more duck puns, the team begins paddling upstream, gaining in confidence with every stroke, and gathering quite a speed.

One thing that Mallard neglected to teach his group is how to stop. Garganey, Gadwall, Pintail, Shoveler and Wigeon shoot under the brick arch into Watermill gardens, suddenly confronting unknown territory, and an alien giant peering down menacingly, the plum sauce monster every duck is taught to fear.

"Thrust your paddle deep in the water," shouts Mallard from the other side of the arch, annoyed with his oversight, "and push forwards."

"And shift your weight by moving your bottom," orders Eider, giving a knowing look to her advanced group, "but whatever you do, don't roll over."

Like some sort of splash fest, the five novices somehow navigate back under the brick arch, spurred on by copious amounts of adrenalin running through their veins to escape capture and inevitable wrapping in a pancake!

•

"Is that you, Lorna?" enquires Harry, collecting wood from a new pile accumulating in the far corner of Lancaster Cottage garden, just beyond the red apple tree. He knows this will bring the wrath of Travis and Purrkins if they ever find out, but given their rising prices, it is a risk worth taking.

"Hi, Harry," replies Lorna, hiding deep inside the woodpile, nestling in dried leaves. "What are you doing in this neck of the woods?"

"Nothing, Lorna. Nothing at all," Harry responds somewhat prickly, caught red-handed taking wood, changing the subject as he tries to hide the swag behind his back. "Lovely apples, aren't they?"

"Yes, they are, Harry," agrees Lorna, following Harry's gaze to the low hanging fruit, out of reach but tempting, nonetheless. "Don't worry, Harry. I won't mention anything to Travis or

Purrkins. I may be a snake in the grass and a grass snake to boot, but a grassing snake I am not!"

"What brings you here?" asks Harry, only knowing Lorna to say hello to and no more, takes the chance to get to know her better. "I only ever see you in the diner."

"I always go for a long swim late afternoon after closing the diner," details Lorna, happy to have company for a change. "Then I like to dry off in the sun before exploring the gardens, keeping abreast of any changes and noting anything of interest. I was a little tired and came across this makeshift den with its enticing duvet of dead leaves and thought I'd grab forty winks before heading home."

"I'm building an extension at home," explains Harry, resting his weary feet and perching on a protruding branch, "and Rodin mentioned this growing pile of untapped wood, so I thought I could save a few pennies."

"Good idea," nods Lorna, knowing the mark-up Travis and Pekins charge. "Pennies to the poor are like pounds to the prosperous."

"Exactly, Lorna, and when you come from nothing," adds Harry, rationally, "you have nothing to lose."

Harry and Lorna chew the late afternoon fat, swapping stories and anecdotes, Harry agreeing to build a canopy on the diner and Lorna accepting an invitation to dinner when Harry's extension is complete. Time is lost in conversation. The yapping pair are oblivious to Red Wellies, suddenly a few yards away, picking an apple, the crunch of the first bite alerting them to the nearby threat.

"Red Wellies!" Harry and Lorna shout simultaneously, diving for cover inside the woodpile, Harry rolling into a ball and Lorna coiling into a spiral like a mouldy green pain au raisin.

"Are you okay, Harry?" whispers Lorna, trying to spy Red Wellies.

"Yeah. I'm okay, Lorna," responds Harry, realising he has stupidly left his tool bag outside. "We must keep perfectly still. Red Wellies is bound to go any minute."

A shadow casts over the woodpile as Red Wellies, a fire-starter and creator of an accidental funeral pyre, ignites a hot, burning and cremating inferno, partly disguised by intoxicating and suffocating smoke. Every garden inhabitant's worst nightmare.

"We need to get out, Lorna," says Harry, weighing up the alternatives. "Or we'll be burnt alive."

"We can't leave, Harry," replies Lorna, confronting two evils as the smoke places a deadly hand over her face. "Red Wellies will get us."

Fortuitously, Rodin flies over to select a piece of wood for his latest sculpture, a commission for Lord and Lady Bird's new salon. Frightened by the appearance of Red Wellies and about to head home, he notices Harry's abandoned tool bag, but no sign of Harry. As the smoke wafts higher and higher, consuming the entire corner of the garden, including Red Wellies and the apple tree, Rodin fears the worst. Imagining his friend trapped inside the woodpile and unable to escape the inevitable, Rodin finds the nearest tree just outside the boundary wall.

Tapping in code, Rodin spells out, G_E_T / O_U_T / N_O_W / H_A_R_R_Y / W_H_I_L_E / I / D_I_S_T_R_A_C_T / R_E_D / W_E_L_L_I_E_S.

Hearing the message, Harry and Lorna make a break for the nearest red rose bush while Red Wellies searches in vain for the location of Rodin and his distinctive knocking. Just as the woodpile erupts into a volcano of flames, devouring everything with a voraciousness previously unseen, and spitting fire like a gobby footballer.

"I thought we were toast, Lorna!" Harry sighs relief, picking up his tool bag containing a lifetime's collection on the way.

"Worse than that, Harry," jokes Lorna, trying to make light of the near-miss, "I thought I was a snakebiting the dust!"

They both laugh, nervously, knowing how close a call this is.

•

Queen Vespula, referred to as Queen V by her distant cousin, Queen B, stands before an atrium full of subjects, an assorted crew of yellow jacket wasps, joined by a handful of foreign dignitaries and a contingent of visiting French hornets. Alongside is committed companion and confidante to Queen V, Prince Dauber, and heiress, Princess Wasperella.

It is the grand opening of the much-awaited new palace, designed by Italian architect, Vespa Velutina, VV for short, erected in a prime location at the top of an imposing red apple tree, overlooking red rosebushes with stunning views across Watermill Stream and beyond. Branded, The Barb, this iconic landmark combines state of the art, lightweight cladding with the ancient oriental art of origami to create a translucent paper masterpiece intended to house the entire colony under one roof. Complete with dining, sports and entertainment facilities, this complex network of interlocking cells presents space in a highly innovative way, specifically to encourage work, rest and play.

"Before I declare The Barb open," begins Queen V, standing in front of the majestic staircase with a primed pair of scissors to cut the red ribbon. "I would like to invite the architect to say a few words about the inspiration behind our impressive new palace and our permanent new home."

Queen V gestures to VV, who is wearing an outlandish creation to echo The Barb, a see-through paper dress, cleverly unrevealing, faceted by origami folds of angling planes to disguise the body's natural contours, and radiating from within, black and yellow. Wings are angelic and decorated in small white petals posed to frame her jet-black bouffant hair. Topped by pièce de résistance, a fantastic pair of dark sunglasses, and toed with high heel silver corn husk shaped shoes, all adding to the mystique known as VV.

Queen V feels somewhat underdressed, wearing a bright yellow and black hoop twin set woollen suit with matching accessories, a string of pearls and crowned with a yellow hat. Wings elegantly tinted black and neatly tucked away, unassuming and understated. Still, Queen V is in her twilight years and relies on pomp rather than ceremony for attention.

Princess Wasperella, on the other hand, exudes natural beauty with piercing dark eyes, gorgonising and spellbinding. She effortlessly wears an elegant black and gold dress to emphasise her extended height and long legs, and wings dusted in gold glitter like a sun-blessed goddess. Prince Dauber is suited and booted in a uniform yellow jacket, differentiated by medals of honour presented for bravery during yesteryear skirmishes.

VV breaks etiquette, and air kisses Queen V on both cheeks, performing, "Moi. Moi," for everyone to hear. Queen V remains stoic, not wishing to embarrass VV during her moment of glory.

"Your highness, distinguished guests, ladies and gentlemen, monsieurs et madames," formally acknowledges VV, motioning with both arms like a cabaret singer engaging an audience. "Welcome to my most important and relevant work to date – The Barb. As the name suggests, it delivers with a sting, gets beneath the surface and never lets go," describes VV, knurling her fingers for effect and emphasis, jesting, "at least, not without tweezers anyway!

"Inspired by my time in the Far East, studying under the late great visionary, Yakitori San, I have come to realise that buildings are only as good as the communities they serve. Our Asian counterparts coexist because of their exemplary goodwill towards one another. Harmony relies on an ability to live side by side, abiding by the rules, however petty some might seem, and by instigating impeccable manners and mutual respect for one's neighbours. The Barb is the perfect tool to perpetuate this philosophy. Remember, The Barb is just that, a tool, and you are its users, able to adapt and shape to suit your personal peculiarities and characteristics.

"What you then say, or do behind closed doors is up to you," jokes VV, realising that she is receiving blank stares, adding uncharacteristically and self-deprecating, "unless of course, the walls are paper thin!"

General chatter follows a round of applause, Queen V thanking VV and her talented team, and of course, the group of engineers, without whom none of this would be possible.

"Thank you, VV, very enlightening," smiles Queen V, curtly, adding with a hint of venom and a sting in her tail, "and by neighbours, you refer to everyone here today. Not our frightful neighbours on the other side of Watermill Stream. That sanctimonious Queen B and her infuriating workers with no regard for territory, thinking that it is acceptable to invade our terrain as if they have the sole right to our red roses, our pollen and our nectar. Taking what justifiably belongs to us as if somehow, they are so much more important. It is sheer and utter arrogance!"

The yellow jackets cheer with equal venom and disdain, chanting Queen V's name over and over like over-patriotic hooligans.

VV throws in the towel at this losing battle, rolling her eyes behind dark glasses, luckily from view, muttering under breath, "What was I expecting? A wasp never changes its stripes."

Queen V delights in her loyal support, safe in the knowledge that she can call on this unfaltering allegiance whenever needed, even against Red Wellies if necessary, and that her devotees will always protect The Barb from harm, or at least go down fighting. Prince Dauber stands proudly behind Queen V, nodding while Princess Wasperella closes her eyes, purses her lips and shakes her head in exasperation at this continuous and ridiculous feuding.

"So, without further ado," concludes Queen V, controlling and commanding silence as she cuts the ribbon in two, "I declare The Barb open and ready for business."

Everyone follows Queen V upstairs, eager to explore the unveiling spectacle, keen to claim first dibs on accommodation, disappointed when cells are pre-appointed and following a natural hierarchy according to social positioning and significance to Queen V.

Queen V stops in her tracks, sniffing the air like a bloodhound detecting a scent. "Can anyone smell smoke?"

There is no need for an answer as smoke seeps through every joint, supposedly airtight, unearthing cut corners and subquality cladding and detoured funds into internal trim and fancy fittings.

"How can this be?" exclaims VV, blaming the engineers, her reputation in tatters.

"I blame you, VV," says Queen V, pointing her finger directly and wagging as if VV is a disobedient child. "Style over substance. You and your airy-fairy visions. Get out of my sight."

Calm converts to complete chaos in a matter of seconds, everyone scrambling for the emergency exits, unfamiliar with their whereabouts, not yet drilled in fire procedures. Screaming and disorder prevail as the hierarchy goes out of the window, replaced by anarchy, workers falling underfoot, trampled in the stampede, an angry mob boiling over with unrestrained rage, spilling out from a singular exit.

"Over there," sounds a French hornet, signalling towards the smoking source. "It's Red Wellies."

"And over there," sounds another French hornet, louder and longer. "Worker bees are stealing our red rose nectar again."

"You know what you have to do," orders Queen V, overlooking from an outside balcony, breathing a sigh of relief that the smoke is from an external fire and not from inside the palace as first feared. "Take no prisoners."

VV makes a hasty exit while the coast is clear, her shortcomings well and truly exposed. She thanks her lucky stars to live a solitary life away from this dysfunctional social organisation that breeds its unhealthy strain of toxicity and destruction.

Red Wellies swats and waves like King Kong hanging from the Empire State, mostly missing, occasionally backhanding a yellow jacket to the floor to dust down then come back more aggressive and virulent.

The smoke hinders progress, screening potential victims, although its effects are immediate on inhalation, calming the warring wasps but critically rendering the bees open targets.

Fights erupt all around as yellow jackets pound female worker bees into the ground. An unfair match with no referee and no one to end the carnage until it's too late, lifeless bodies are strewn all about, the rampaging wasps retreating to celebrate victory as the smoke subsides, some carrying trophy souvenirs.

Thankfully unharmed but covered in the blood of her compatriots, Princess Wannabee returns to B Hive, tears rolling down her cheeks, losing count of the casualties to report back. More questions than answers fly around inside her head, mixing with both instinctive revenge and disappointment towards her attackers and the worrying level of ensconced ignorance.

•

"TTT_Try this one, Mumble," says Stutter, perching on a young succulent growing in the Lancaster Cottage potting shed, Mumble and Stutter accidentally stumbling inside during their bud crawl that began hours ago close to home in the York Cottage potting shed.

Today is Mumble's hatchday. Everything was going fine until Stutter suggested crossing Watermill Stream to savour a few flowers on the other side, hearing that there were some great local nectars in the red rose garden. Starting fresh and smartly dressed, now Mumble and Stutter are dishevelled and unkempt, covered from head to toe in pollen, hair dripping and shirts stained with spilt nectar.

"Mmm," replies Mumble, downing the nectar as if there is no tomorrow. "How many have we had?"

"I've lll_lost count," admits Stutter, attempting to count the flowers on his fingers, "but I've never tasted anything like it."

"Me neither!" states Mumble, trying not to fall off another budding red rose, proclaiming in between burps. "I love you, bumble! You're the best!"

"I lll_love you, ttt_too, bumble!" echoes Stutter, trying to focus, seeing double. "We're like ppp_peas in a ppp_pod!"

"Like partridges in a pear tree!" adds Mumble, racking his brain for more similes. "Like Jack and Jill, who went up the hill!"

"And came ttt_tumbling down!" finishes Stutter, holding onto Mumble as they stumble around, straining to work out which way is home.

"Over here," shouts Mumble, guiding Stutter down a blind alley. "Oops. Maybe not."

"WWW_What about this way," suggests Stutter, luckily and quite accidentally, dragging Mumble towards the potting shed door which miraculously opens. Neither Mumble nor Stutter sees Red Wellies, in their determination to find freedom, staggering in a stupor, reeking of nectar and covered in yet more pollen.

"Let's get back to where we started, Stutter," suggests Mumble, leading Stutter to Watermill Stream in time for the last ferry. "Perhaps we can catch the last buds before they close for the day!"

"Great idea, MMM_Mumble," nods Stutter, combing his hair without a mirror into a ridiculous centre parting. "It is your hhh_hatchday, after all, singing without stuttering,
Ha_bee hatchday to you,
Ha_bee hatchday to you,
Ha_bee hatchday bumble Mumble,
Ha_bee hatchday to you!"

•

"Queen V may have won the battle, spelt B_A_T_T_L_E," says Queen B, sending for Spit and Polish to tend to Princess Wannabee, "but if it's a war she wants then it's a war she's going to get."

"This isn't the answer, mother," reasons Princes Wannabee, handing her blood-soaked outfit to Spit from behind a screen. "Fighting fire with fire will only end in more tears and more deaths," taking a towel from Polish.

"What do you think, Buzz?" asks Queen B while Princess Wannabee showers. "You have your ear closer to the ground than me, spelt C_L_O_S_E_R."

"Of course, Princess Wannabee's right, honey," responds Wannabee, adopting her pet name after pronouncing their love so publicly, "but if you don't stand up to Queen V, then she will continue to walk over you."

"Give that persistent, annoying wasp an inch, spelt I_N_C_H," concurs Queen B, searching her phone for the S.P.I.N number and dialling, "and she'll take a mile, spelt M_I_L_E."

"S.P.I.N," answers Freckles, unable to see that the incoming call is from Queen B.

"Freckles, it's me. Queen B," announces Queen B, holding her hand over the mouthpiece momentarily and asking Buzz to fetch King Fisher to discuss Queen V.

"Long time no see," replies Freckles, oblivious to her innocent blunder. "How can I be of service, ma'am?"

"Queen V has crossed the line, spelt L_I_N_E," exclaims Queen B, determination growing on her face, "and she needs putting in her place, spelt P_L_A_C_E."

"I had heard things on the grapevine about territory and the rights to the roses," admits Freckles, before making another unintentional blooper, "but I didn't see this coming."

"I need S.P.I.N to do a reconnaissance of her new palace, spelt P_A_L_A_C_E," instructs Queen V, nodding at Buzz as he gives the thumbs up, "and find out what you can."

"Very good, ma'am," replies Freckles, pressing the S.P.I.N alert button. "We're onto it straight away."

"And Freckles," continues Queen B, determination turning to resignation.

"Yes, ma'am?" enquires Freckles.

"From this point onwards, spelt O_N_W_A_R_D_S," declares Queen B, decisively, just as Princess Wannabee exits the shower and shakes her head in disagreement. "We are at war with the wasps, spelt W_A_R."

5
Roses are red!

Rosewall is a medieval market village with an extra-wide high street to cater for bygone horse-drawn carts and waggons, swelling around a late Georgian central marketplace addition. This focal freestanding building, complete with four-piece clock tower and golden dragon weathervane, is the setting for duelling florists, York and Lancaster Blooms. Previously, one substantial florist, accessed both ends to create a thoroughfare for village folk to shortcut through, to shelter from the elements, or more importantly, to enjoy and to purchase the beautiful flowers on sale. Now divided in two, York Blooms faces south, and Lancaster Blooms faces north, with a central brick wall preventing through access, extending to both floors up to the slate roof. As such, never the twain shall meet, including customers, deliveries, and any passers-by.

Primrose exploits the south-facing aspect, converting the second floor into York Blooms Café and spilling out on to the front pavement with white bistro tables and chairs and several overhanging white canvas umbrellas as the go-to tea and coffee shop in Rosewall. The serene, subtle white interior tones provide the perfect setting as the sun moves west to east, the white roses possessing a tranquillity worthy of their delicate scent, wafting over every sitter like the sensual hands of an aromatherapy masseur. Primrose diversifies into contemporary gifts and knick-knacks, deliberately positioned for added temptation. She sells honey from heaven and Ann Neville's rainbow jam to take away or drizzled and dolloped over freshly baked scones, English teacakes and seeded granary toast, accompanied by signature Indian cupcakes from none other than Mrs Stanley.

Primrose manages the florists with her notorious white roses, while Pearl and Matt White, sister and brother and old school chums, run the café, standing in for Primrose whenever necessary.

Rosemary, whether by default or by choosing the short straw, inhabits the north-facing side, which benefits from uniform light throughout the day, and is less affected by the heat of the sun that can over-wilt cut flowers. Still, the shade is less alluring to customers in search of a hot beverage or a place to sit as an office away from home. However hard Rosemary tries to make a rival tea shop, then a coffee shop, then a tea and coffee shop, and more lately, an oriental tea ceremony shop, the public appeal is never quite the same.

Exhausted with trying too hard, Rosemary takes a step back and a long look at her shop. The strategic lighting shows off her prize-winning roses like warm coals on a winters night, alluring and seductive all year round. Even the aroma matches the mood magnificently, being earthier and fuller-bodied like a vintage red wine or a pedigree bloodline.

"What can I do to compete with Primrose?" Rosemary asks her long-standing assistant, Crimson, as they stand outside sipping coffee from red mugs awaiting next customers. "I have the best flowers, but she has that added attraction."

"How about a South American coffee shop?" suggests Crimson, sipping her flat white that exudes Columbian, "With some of that Latin passion and fire!"

"I don't want gimmick, Crimson," responds Rosemary, straining not to drown any seed of an idea. "I want something that compliments my red roses or the colour red."

"Sex!" blurts Crimson from nowhere, blushing a little as she peers at Rosemary over her glasses while sipping more coffee.

"Is that a request or a suggestion, Crimson?" Rosemary says rhetorically and semi-joking, immediately countering with, "I'm not turning the second floor into a tart's boudoir or Rosewall's answer to suburban swinging!"

"I mean sexy, then!" refines Crimson, searching *sexy* on her phone and showing Rosemary before she has a chance to edit, "Something like this."

"I don't call a middle-aged man in a red leather thong, sexy," mocks Rosemary, almost in tears with laughter, "and I'm not selling women's undies!"

"Not undies!" ridicules Crimson, shaking her head in desperation. "Lingerie, specifically *ladies* lingerie," taking a bar of chocolate from her pocket. "Fancy a piece? It's ultra-dark and goes down a treat with a morning coffee or an afternoon brew."

"Ladies lingerie," whispers Rosemary, popping a piece of chocolate into her mouth and mulling over Crimson's suggestion. "Lingerie for ladies. Lingerie for the lady. Lancaster Lingerie. Mmm, this is good, Crimson."

"Thank you, Rosemary," replies Crimson, pleased with her suggestion. "Women love lingerie."

"Not the lingerie, Crimson," dismisses Rosemary, feeling like Archimedes running from his bath after his eureka moment, except fully clothed, thankfully. "The chocolate, Crimson. The bloody brilliant chocolate."

"Oh, I see, Rosemary!" responds Crimson, slightly dejected before sharing Rosemary's enthusiasm, stating, "Women love chocolate."

"They most certainly do, Crimson," builds Rosemary, letting her imagination run wild, "as their secret guilty pleasure. And if they don't, then the men love to hoover up!"

"Chocolates are a perfect companion and compliment for our red roses," acknowledges Crimson, offering more chocolate to fuel the ideas, slipping in as an aside. "Lancaster bouquets and boxes."

"Picture this, Crimson," imagines Rosemary, relaying her vison as she swallows melting chocolate. "Like perfection that is a Lancaster red rose, unbranded, distinguished by its colour, shape and scent alone, Lancaster chocolates will be in an unbranded box. Except that this is no ordinary box, this is the purest red box, seamlessly square and the perfect depth, forever referred to as just *red chocolates*, only available at Lancaster Blooms so by default, Lancaster red chocolates to accompany Lancaster red roses.

"And inside the red box is a rose-shaped red velvet tray, beautifully displaying each chocolate like a persuasive petal, every masterpiece made by the devil's hand, and a gamble of Russian Roulette."

"Are the chocolates red, Rosemary?" asks Crimson, trying to keep up.

"They're all dark chocolate and carrying the scent of a red rose," replies Rosemary, clarifying, "but everyone will call them red roses that come in a red box."

"And what flavours are they?" enquires Crimson, salivating at the thought. "There has to be one made with South American coffee."

"What is it with you and South American coffee, Crimson," teases Rosemary, following a new customer in-store. "It doesn't matter what flavour they are. It just matters that they are great quality in great packaging with a great brand and a great name or as in our case, a great brand with no name!

"And we can have chocolate bars with similar plain red packaging," continues Rosemary, on a roll after selling four dozen Lancaster roses, "and sell the richest, darkest hot or cold chocolate, Crimson."

"Available in five distinctive flavours," builds Crimson, salivating at the mere thought, "to represent the number of petals on a Lancaster rose."

"And five being the number of digits on your hand," details Rosemary, holding out an outstretched hand, then another. "Perfect in decimalisation, being divisible into ten."

"Harmony in numbers, Rosemary," summarises Crimson, perplexed by the relevance to chocolate.

"Echoing the five senses relating to the eyes, ears, skin, nose, and mouth," expands Rosemary, "and the perceptions of vision, hearing, touch, smell, and taste."

"Oh, this is fun, Rosemary," declares Crimson, offering to make another coffee. "When do we start?"

"Immediately, Crimson," smiles Rosemary, rubbing her hands as if hatching a dastardly plan of revenge. "I'm going to call my branding guru and my architect as soon as I finish my cup of coffee."

•

"I want this whole wall to be a continuous chocolate waterfall," Rosemary briefs Redmond, the architect, pointing to the dividing wall. "Behind glass so that kids don't stick their grubby little fingers in, or adults for that matter!"

"We'll have to do it in sections," explains Redmond, tape measuring the length. "I suggest three."

"Can't we have just one big one?" enquires Rosemary, imagining an ill-fitting toupee.

"Don't worry, Rosemary," placates Redmond, scribbling in his sketchbook, "you won't see the join."

Redmund is the only architect in the village, consequently in high demand, often torn between commitments, and balancing allegiances. He walks a delicate tightrope when working with Primrose or Rosemary, navigating their unerring rivalry and one-upmanship, in fear of upsetting one or other, forever treading on eggshells.

"Then I want a circular window in the floor for a birds-eye view of my beautiful red roses below," states Rosemary, twirling on the floor with arms outstretched like Wonder woman.

"All glass?" asks Redmond, laying his tape measure on the floor to mark out six foot.

"No glass, Redmond," corrects Rosemary, rethinking her description. "Think of it as a viewing gallery, encircled by red velvet seating extending to a safe height to meet all the standards and regulations that I am sure you are going to bore me with!"

"That should be possible," responds Redmond, ignoring Rosemary's remark, complimenting, "and look fantastic, Rosemary."

"Then a bank of refrigerated display cabinets both sides," continues Rosemary, pointing left and right, "lit with state-of-the-art red LEDs that magically react to daylight levels for a constant glow, to show off my precious red chocolates. "

"Cool!" Redmond says simply, joking, "or should I say, hot!"

"And then, Redmond," proclaims Rosemary, signalling like an aircraft marshaller, "I want everything to be red. Glorious, adorable red!"

"I expected nothing less, Rosemary," responds Redmund, reaching into his black leather designer satchel to retrieve a professional colour swatch folder. "But there's red, and there's red!"

"I want Lancaster red," requests Rosemary, flicking through the folder as if viewing a page by page hand-drawn animation.

"Lancaster red?" puzzles Redmund, taking back the folder to find the relevant colour swatch. "I've not heard of that one before."

"You won't have done, Redmund," replies Rosemary, smiling as she pulls out a red rose from her pocket like a conjurer hiding something up a sleeve. "We will match my Lancaster red rose for the perfect and most potent red, fittingly referred to as Lancaster red."

6
Secret service and preparation for war!

Princess Wasperella takes an evening stroll, in need of respite from her plotting mother and yearning for some me-time to let her hair down. She knows a down to earth cocktail bar on the right bank, not too far from home, called Dolicho, run by transvespulas, Dronny and Dyetee, serving seasonal fruit concoctions throughout the summer. Frequented by local fireflies and glow worm couples, this charming establishment inside a disused squirrel store pulsates to the sound of the summertime blues.

"Give me one of your Squamosas, Dronny," orders Princess Wasperella, disguising as *Wella* in a yellow gold wig to avoid paparazzi and annoying stalkers from The Barb, "and make it a strong one!"

"Coming right up, Wella," confirms Dronny, juggling fruit with Dyetee behind the bar and filling a cocktail shaker, adding more fermented apple juice than usual. "Tough day?"

"You don't want to hear about it, Dronny," dismisses Princess Wasperella, swivelling on her stool to admire the live band. Lennon on the piano, Dylan on trombone, Thomas on trumpet and Clarice as lead singer. "That's a great sound they've got going."

"You ain't heard nothing yet," raves Dronny, placing the Squamosa on the bar and lighting grated orange peel for effect. "When they get going, the brass section is on fire!

"There you go, Wella. Get your proboscis into that."

•

"The target is in position, M8," advises F8 by radio, dangling from an overhanging willow to watch Dolicho from across Watermill Stream, "Operation Sting is all systems go."

"The band has been briefed, M8," informs R8, floating slowly downstream on a supped-up speed leaf, driven by B8. "But watch out for Dronny and Dyetee. We think they might be working undercover for Queen V."

"Roger that, R8 and F8," responds M8, brushing his hair, checking his breath and adjusting his tie. "I'm going in."

"And M8," adds R8, unable to make contact. "M8. Come in, M8. Do you read me?"

"M8 has turned off his equipment, R8," advises B8, shaking his head and steering the speed leaf back to base. "You know what M8's like about working alone."

"He just better watch what he drinks," says R8, despairing at M8's recklessness. "Those cocktails can be lethal."

•

M8 enters Dolicho, clocking the band and surveying the bar for quick exits and the toilet. He is bursting!

"I'll have an Apple Tartini, please," orders M8, after ablutions and strolling casually to the bar, standing deliberately close to Princess Wasperella. "Shaken not stirred. I can't stand all that fruit getting in the way, and definitely, no olives!"

M8 sips his drink and listens to the band, reaching for a cigarette and searching his pockets for a lighter.

"Sorry, sir," informs Dyetee, pointing to a tiny sign behind the bar. "No smoking. You must go outside if you want to partake."

"Filthy habit!" remarks Princess Wasperella, rather arrogantly and waspish.

"That's very caring of you, Ms..?" responds M8, delighted to get such an easy inroad, prompting Princess Wasperella for her name.

"Wella," offers Princess Wasperella, glancing at M8 then returning her gaze to the band. "Wella Ware."

"I'm sure you are," comments M8, a tad mocking, putting away his cigarette. "As you are Wella Ware, I've been trying to give it up, but it's one of those nights!"

"Tell me about it, Mr..?" softens Princess Wasperella, turning to M8 with questioning eyebrows, not registering the bitter tongue in cheek reference to lemonade despite M8's feeble impression.

"The name's, Cadd. Connor Cadd," answers M8, assuming a regular identity, and emulating his fictional hero and role model.

"Good evening, Mr Cadd," greets Princess Wasperella, smiling as she reprimands, "you do know the smoking ban has existed for many years!"

"Call me, Connor," corrects M8, ignoring to comment, taking Princess Wasperella's drink with one hand, wrapping another around her waist and pointing to the dancefloor with a third. "Let's dance, Wella?"

"Do I have a choice?" asks Princess Wasperella, unresisting. "You assume too much, Mr Cadd...Connor."

"It'll help take our minds off our worries," says M8, swinging Princess Wasperella around the dancefloor and sweeping her off her feet. "But I have to warn you. I have four left feet!"

M8 and Princess Wasperella dance the night away, lost in each other's arms. Clarice warbles tune after tune in her inimitable style, changing costumes several times, each time more outrageous and forever the drama drag queen. As predicted, Dylan and Thomas warm the audience to fever pitch while Lennon, transported to Lalaland, improvises and steers the tempo as if playing with twice as many fingers.

"My goodness!" exclaims Princess Wasperella, spotting the clock when they find a booth during yet another intermission. "I didn't realise the time."

"Don't tell me your name's not Wella," says M8, seeing Princess Wasperella's face change from one of horror to one of relief when he jokes, "and I've been hanging out with Cinderella all night."

"Oh, Connor," smiles Princess Wasperella, kissing M8 on the cheek and getting up to leave, "I'm not turning into a pumpkin if that's what you mean, but I really must be getting home."

"Let me escort you, Wella," insists M8, helping Princess Wasperella with her coat. "Who knows who's hanging about at this time of night."

"I'm a big girl, Connor," rejects Princess Wasperella, buttoning her coat. "I can look after myself."

"I don't doubt that for a moment," retorts M8, retrieving no useful information throughout the evening and worrying that Operation Sting is a failure. "When can I see you again?" M8 persists before she has the chance to answer. "Meet me outside here at midday. I know a great restaurant downstream."

"Very well, Connor," accepts Princess Wasperella, falling for M8's charm and not wanting him to uncover her true identity by escorting her home. "Sounds divine."

"I look forward to it, Wella Ware," whispers M8, watching Princess Wasperella exit, realising a mutual attraction, correcting, "or should I say, Princess Wasperella."

•

"I thought you were going to stand me up," says M8, jumping to attention and greeting the fashionably late Princess.

"This is what I call being on time!" replies Princess Wasperella, still disguising as Wella with a yellow gold wig beneath a flowing wide-brim black hat to compliment her elegant black summer dress, shimmering with fine gold flake.

"You look stunning, Wella," compliments M8, taking her hand and leading down to Watermill Steam's edge. "Please, allow me."

M8 helps Princess Wasperella onto the speed leaf, moored to the Dolicho jetty. "Meet my butler, Bates," M8 introduces Princess Wasperella to B8 at the helm, who gives him a disapproving look.

B8 is under strict orders not to let M8 out of his sight, reluctantly agreeing to act as chauffeur, also untrusting of

M8 to handover the speed leaf for fear of never seeing its return, or at least in one piece.

"It's a little off the beaten track," describes M8, ordering B8 to go faster, who then deliberately rocks the leaf to spill champulp over M8's legs. "It's a two-star Mitch & Lynn restaurant called The Ratz. The ground-breaking brown rat owners moved their successful city establishment here when their chef, an overweight duck named Bray, wanted to move back to the country."

"Is it far?" asks Princess Wasperella, coming to M8's rescue with a handkerchief from one of her handbags.

"Just where Watermill Stream joins the river," outlines M8, resuming interplay after drying his legs as best as he can.

"I've never left Watermill before," admits Wasperella, feeling decadent and rebellious. "How exciting."

•

"Welcome, M8," quacks Bray, waddling out to greet M8. "We have your usual table waiting."

"M8?" Princess Wasperella asks M8, also reeling from the *usual table* comment.

"He means, mate, don't you Bray?" replies M8, awkwardly trying to conceal the schoolboy error.

"Yes, yes. Of course, mate!" corrects Bray, mopping the sweat from his brow and shifting uncomfortably in his chef's tunic, overcompensating, "Connor, how lovely to see you again, Mr Cadd. It's been so long. We should have a table for you!"

M8 and Princess Wasperella are shown to a table while Bray disappears into the kitchen. The dining room is full of an eclectic mix of business, leisure and romantic lunchers, some reserved and incognito, others loud and brash. The stilted restaurant juts out across the stream, buckling under the combined weight of covers as the swan's legs paddle faster than usual to provide the first-class culinary experience everyone has come to expect from The Ratz. The spectacular view distracts from any tardy or less than perfect plate, stretching towards the river, the stream spilling into and immediately swallowed by the more massive expanse.

"My name is Kismet, and I'll be your waiter today," announces F8, dressed as a waiter, handing M8 and Princess Wasperella a menu. "Would sir like to see the wine list? I can recommend the Gypsy Mothschild. A nomadic and free-spirited wine with earthy undertones."

"*Madam* would like to see the wine list," interjects Princess Wasperella, playing second fiddle to no one, even when disguised as Wella or dining with someone she likes. "The Mothschild is overpriced and overrated. We'll have the Watermill garden red."

"Excellent choice," responds F8, giving M8 a sly wink and trying not to express delight in M8's dressing down. "Very cheeky on the palate, madam!"

Course follows course and the garden red flows. M8 spins many a yarn with a web of white lies, seeking to put Princess Wasperella at ease and to coax her into his elaborate sting.

"I have a confession, Wella," discloses M8, undertaking every which way but loose to break down her façade of steel. "I am not who you think I am!"

"What do you mean?" asks Princes Wasperella, sitting bolt upright, and attracting strange stares from fellow diners.

"The speed leaf," reveals M8, doing his utmost to win acting awards. "It's not mine. I borrowed it from my friend who did me a favour and pretended to be my butler."

"I had my suspicions," smiles Princess Wasperella, pointing to the now dry champulp stains.

"And the meal," continues M8, laying down his last hand, "Bray and I are old school buddies. He always gives me mate's rates."

"Why did you see the need to lie?" enquires Princess Wella, uncomfortably hiding her own deception. "Do you think I'm that shallow?"

"I wanted to impress," replies M8, shaking his head. "You are so glamorous and gorgeous, while everyone has a genuine phobia for spiders, despising our every move with loud vocal threats, misunderstanding and jumping to conclusions based on our ungainly and gangly appearance."

"Some spiders can be quite frightening," responds Princess Wasperella, placing her hands on his, "but not you, Connor. You're sweet and funny and talented, and I like you very much."

"Thank you, Wella," says M8, smiling modestly then speaking honestly from the bottom of his heart, lowering his guard and breaking protocol. "You are not like other wasps. You are kind, considerate and level-headed, and I like you, too. A lot."

"Wasps are also heavily misunderstood," suggests Princess Wasperella, taking a deep breath. "But while we are on the subject of telling the truth, I also have a confession," she continues, removing her yellow gold wig and shaking out her long black hair. "I am not Wella Ware. My name is Princess Wasperella. My mother is Queen V, my father is Prince Dauber, and I live in The Barb. There, I've spilt the beans."

M8 says nothing, smiling on the inside but growing uneasy with this premeditated entrapment, B8 shouting down his earpiece. "The target's taken the bait, M8. Now reel her in."

•

"Thank you for coming, King Fisher, spelt C_O_M_I_N_G," says Queen B, convening in the hexagonal drawing-room and signalling Spit and Polish to serve afternoon tea and to bring a pot of B Hive's purest honey, reserved for dignitaries and special occasions. "Do pass on my best wishes to Queen Fishnette. It's ages since we last got together, spelt A_G_E_S."

"She has taken Prince Fishin and Princess Fishelle to Shelduck Summer Camp," details King Fisher, taking advantage of his royal status and helping himself to spoonsful of honey, much to the annoyance of Buzz who rarely gets an opportunity. "In an attempt to excite them about our traditions and to teach them how to fish. Something for which they show great contempt and a distinct lack of interest, more focussed on screens and social media."

"You were once like that, Wannabee, spelt O_N_C_E," says Queen B, empathising with King Fisher, regrettably awakening the beast.

"I still am!" replies Princess Wannabee, belligerently, always looking for a chance to wind up her mother. "What is it with everyone's fixation for the past? Dinosaurs became extinct because they didn't see what was coming!"

Queen B ignores her daughter and nods at Buzz, urging him to tuck in before King Fisher finishes the pot. King Fisher grimaces at the sight of Buzz drizzling the last drop and luckily refraining from licking the pot.

"Colonel Rant has arrived, honey," announces Buzz, quickly correcting to, "your highness," after seeing King Fisher chuckle. "He's waiting in reception."

"Please ask the doorbee to escort Colonel Rant, Buzz, spelt R_A_N_T," requests Queen B with a loving glance.

"Certainly, ma'am," responds Buzz, reciprocating and contacting reception.

Queen B recalls the last meeting when Colonel Rant and King Fisher nearly came to blows, typically poles apart over any correct course of action.

"Please be patient with Colonel Rant, your highness," Queen B addresses King Fisher diplomatically. "We know how contrary our fellow ants can be. Anti-this, anti-that, and how Colonel Rant is deliberately obstructive and disagreeable, but we need them on our side, spelt S_I_D_E."

"Colonel Rant is the most jumped-up, argumentative ant, I have ever come across, your highness," reacts King Fisher, realising he has to be the bigger bird. "As you wish, your highness."

"Colonel Rant," announces Spit as in marches Colonel Rant, antagonistically and chest puffed. Immaculately dressed and decorated, an eye-patch distinguishes him further.

"Colonel Rant, ma'am," roars Colonel Rant, stamping to attention and saluting, staring at an imaginary point in space. "At your command, ma'am."

"At ease, Colonel," instructs Queen B, wishing to diffuse the tension immediately. "Cup of tea, spelt T_E_A?"

"Not on duty, ma'am," resists Colonel Rant as Queen B hands him a cup. "Very good, ma'am."

"Take a seat, Colonel," indicates Queen B, considering now to be as good a time as any to begin. "As I explained at our preliminary meeting, we are at war with the wasps, spelt W_A_S_P_S."

"As I also explained previously," reminds King Fisher, avoiding eye contact with Colonel Rant. "I do not want, nor do I see the need for Riverbanks to be drawn into a feud between you and Queen V."

"My Coolstream infantry are up for a fight, ma'am," declares Colonel Rant, eager to steal a march on King Fisher. "Those wasps have it coming."

"Excellent, Colonel, spelt E_X_E_L_L_E_N_T," appreciates Queen B.

"At your service, ma'am," replies Colonel Rant, showing his contempt for King Fisher. "Always ready to defend Queen and country."

"There have been some developments, King Fisher, spelt D_E_V_E_L_O_P_M_E_N_T_S," relates Queen B, prompting Polish to fetch Freckles. "Our friends at S.P.I.N have uncovered some worrying intelligence that will, I am sure, change your mind, spelt C_H_A_N_G_E."

"Freckles, your highness," announces Polish, guiding Freckles to a seat.

"Thank you for coming, Freckles," says Queen B, waiting for Freckles to adjust her chair to face the right direction. "You remember Colonel Rant and King Fisher, spelt F_I_S_H_E_R?"

"Of course, I do, ma'am," replies Freckles, sniffing the air to detect the smell of fish. "King Fisher and I go way back, cooperating to get Riverbanks off the ground and to unravel some hostile takeovers. And Colonel Rant and I are often bumping into each other below ground."

"Hello, Freckles," shouts King Fisher, confusing disabilities, "How lovely to see you again."

"And to see you, too, your highness," responds Freckles, equally booming to prove a point well made.

"Freckles, old bean," states Colonel Rant, studying Freckles up and down in astonishment, taken aback by her untidy and stain-ridden appearance. "It's the first time we've seen each other in daylight."

"Sorry, Colonel," replies Freckles, awkwardly, "but you don't look any different!"

"Now that we have the formalities out of the way, spelt W_A_Y," continues Queen B, resuming control and speaking naturally to require King Fisher to acknowledge his error. "Perhaps Freckles would like to repeat the recent bombshells, spelt B_O_M_B_S_H_E_L_L_S."

"My top Spyders in the field have been monitoring Queen V and The Barb, focusing efforts on Princess Wasperella," begins Freckles, motioning for a cup of tea. "It turns out that this isn't about an ancient feud between bees and wasps, but a battle over the roses, involving total power and supremacy. We know that their code name is Day-V. V for Vendetta, V for Victory, and V for Queen V to reign supreme.

"Queen V is looking to take control of both sides of the garden, including Watermill Stream to rule as a single monarch, eradicating Queen B and controlling everything and everyone within the confines, including King Fisher and Queen Fishnette. Queen V is obsessed with becoming a red and white rose dictator overnight.

"Consequently, she has sent for Monarch Madame Butterfly and Red Admiral Napoleon to come with a fleet, armed to the hilt, and an army of highly skilled grenadier frogs, red jacket wasps and reinforcement French hornets. Meanwhile, Prince Dauber is drilling the yellow jackets in arm-to-arm combat, equipping with deadly weapons and training an elite squad of drones for aerial attacks. Queen V is looking for a short, sharp attack to take everyone by surprise," concludes Freckles, sipping tea, and moving her head side to side for visual effect. "When no one sees her coming."

"You're right, Queen B, this does change everything," admits King Fisher, requesting more tea, staring pensively at the ground. "Who does Queen V think she is?"

"Is it not worth trying to diffuse this diplomatically, mother?" suggests Princess Wannabee at wit's end. "Find a peaceful solution rather than sacrifice hundreds of lives with the possibility of losing everything, forcing an exodus that results in prolonged peril and persecution wherever we go."

"Queen V is a tyrant, Wannabee, spelt T_Y_R_A_N_T," exclaims Queen B, envisaging no other course of action. "A megalomaniac that will stop at nothing."

"With weapons intent on destruction," adds Buzz, looking at Freckles for confirmation, misreading her flinch and embellishing, "with weapons intent on mass destruction."

Princess Wannabee cannot be a party to this madness any longer and exits before she says or does something to regret. She longs for the day when she influences the future, able to preach peace over hate, and common sense over nonsense.

"When do you think Day-V will happen, Freckles?" enquires Colonel Rant, punching his hands in rage, squinting at King Fisher in unexpected solidarity. "Queen V's a loser, that's what she is, King Fisher. A tyrannical loser."

"We have not found out the date, yet," concedes Freckles, shaking her head. "But my Spyders are working on it as we speak."

"So, what do you want us to do, Queen B?" asks King Fisher, caving in to her demands, now that the imminent threat is personal.

"I want everyone from Riverbanks to build a fleet to defend against Monarch Madame Butterfly and Red Admiral Napoleon, spelt D_E_F_E_N_D," instructs Queen B, detailing further, "and to plan and prepare for an all-out attack on Queen V, spelt A_T_T_A_C_K."

"Attack?" queries Colonel Rant, confused, "Don't you mean, defence?"

"We are going to reverse the tables, Colonel, and take the war to Queen V," clarifies Queen B, nodding at Buzz for reassurance, "and catch her by surprise, spelt S_U_R_P_R_I_S_E."

"Excellent decision, ma'am," commends Freckles, enjoying the mounting commitment. "To catch Queen V with her pants down."

"Then all we can do now, spelt N_O_W," concludes Queen B, looking to Spit and Polish, "is have another cup of tea, spelt A_N_O_T_H_E_R."

7
Flooding and fuelling the feud!

Rosemary's red chocolates are the talk of the village, their reputation spreading like juicy gossip to neighbouring towns and beyond. Hordes of visitors flock to see the chocolate waterfall, traipsing up and downstairs like heavily fleeced sheep. Renamed the House of Lancaster, everyone enters fresh-faced and exits wearing chocolate smiles and moustaches, raving about the five flavours of hot chocolate, no one empty-handed, clutching a red box underarm. The red-hot chilli Brazil nut crunch proves to be the most popular, keen eyes and mouths watering for more.

•

"Where is everyone, Pearl?" questions Primrose, coming back inside from the pavement café, usually full but empty again. "We're always chock-a-block on a Friday."

"There can only be one answer," offers Pearl, staring uncomfortably at Matt, who finds something to do upstairs suddenly.

"And what answer is that?" probes Primrose, rearranging the rainbow jam.

"It's next door," replies Pearl, loyal to Primrose but looking forward to lunch when she can dive into the Lancaster pool of chocolate bliss. "Surely, you've heard about the infamous chocolate café?"

"I had heard something," admits Primrose, not telling the truth entirely, "but chocolate's just chocolate, Pearl. The fad will pass."

"I'm not so sure, Primrose," poses Pearl, frank and honest, attempting to divert. "Apparently, *you've never seen or tasted anything like it*, and rumours are rife that Rosemary has cracked it this time."

"Will you go and then report back, Pearl?" requests Primrose, not wanting to give Rosemary the satisfaction of her presence. "Take Matt as if you're on some sort of a family outing."

"I'd love to, Primrose, but you need to go yourself," replies Pearl, avoiding eye contact by turning to cover the usually depleted stack of pastries. "The word on the street is, *it's everything that York Blooms isn't!* It's sultry, naughty, tempting and darn right addictive."

"It sounds like you are talking from experience, Pearl," accuses Primrose with an interrogating look. "Come on. You can be upfront with me."

"Very well, Primrose," begins Pearl, pushed into a corner next to the cash till with no means of escape. "I go every day and have done since its opening three weeks ago. I can't get enough, nor can Matt."

"What's this?" enquires Matt, coming downstairs, thinking the coast is clear. "Do I hear my name spoken in vain?"

"I was just telling Primrose all about the Lancaster chocolate café, Matt," says Pearl, glad to share the burden of truth. "And how good it is."

"It's amazing, Primrose," gushes Matt, opening up like overloaded sluice gates. "You have never tasted hot chocolate like it, and the chocolates, in their striking red box, are to die for! The lavender-scented burnt caramel flavour is my favourite, but there are five flavours to choose from, all out of this world like nothing on earth.

"Imagine Adam and Eve succumbing and savouring the serpent's apple, or a child, biting into a strawberry for the very first time, or having your favourite takeaway after months abroad.

"And the upstairs red chocolate grotto, complete with chocolate waterfall wall, makes you feel like you're in an enchanted chocolate forest in some far-off paradise. It's genius."

Matt stops to swallow the bucket load of overflowing saliva after an over-the-top description and questions his strange choice of comparisons. Pearl continues to nod her head with eyes closed, transported next door with Matt's enthusiasm and five-star recommendation, counting down the time until launch like a bored schoolgirl praying for the last lesson to end.

"It sounds as if I have to experience this for myself," resigns Primrose, left with little choice but to visit Lancaster Blooms for the very first time, sworn never to enter by her late father. "To cross the threshold of bad taste and melodrama into the devil's lair like a weak disciple in betrayal!"

"I wouldn't go that far, Primrose," downplays Pearl, wondering which cousin is the more overdramatic. "It's just a florists selling delicious chocolate!"

•

Primrose swaps her white York Blooms apron for a white linen summer coat, adding a wide-brimmed straw hat complete with white silk band. Although the day is overcast, Primrose wears sunglasses, hoping these will mask her trip to Lancaster Blooms.

Standing in line at the revelation that is the House of Lancaster, Primrose detects the familiar scent of home, the smell of Lancaster red roses drifting along the restless queue, usually battling the bouquet of her York white roses, today breathing in comfort. The upper floor glows red like a burning cauldron, drawing the eye like a bedroom window of the night, signalling its offer and tempting purchase.

Primrose ponders whether to break her paternal promise and to cross the unchartered line or to stand firm and withdraw without harm, her reputation and resilience intact. Just as she pictures her father turning in his grave, Crimson thrusts a free sample in her face, exclaiming, "Goodness me, Primrose. I never thought I'd see the day you entered the House of Lancaster. You must really love chocolate!"

"I was just passing what I thought was Lancaster Blooms, Crimson," fibs Primrose, sampling the slither of red chocolate, "and wondered, why the name change and why the long queue?"

"I hear that your business has taken quite a hit since we opened the Lancaster Chocolate Café and rebranded as the House of Lancaster," announces Crimson, trying but failing to hide her delight. "Red roses and red chocolates somehow stir emotions in the customers that your simple white flowers and cups of tea can only dream to."

"I am not having this conversation with you, Crimson," dismisses Primrose, suppressing anger. "You have spent far too long in the company of that wretched cousin of mine, sprouting ridiculous, uninformed comments, fuelled by ignorance rather than wisdom."

A vision of red appears at the front door to the House of Lancaster, effervescent and ebullient as ever.

"The ground can open up and swallow me now, never to reopen again," bellows Rosemary, just as Primrose is about to make a hasty retreat. "Either my eyes deceive me, or I see two husbands!" she continues, inexplicably quoting Shakespeare as she approaches, clarifying, "My neighbour and my rival, cousin Primrose!"

"Hello, Rosemary," Primrose greets through gritted teeth.

"Hello, Primrose, welcome to the House of Lancaster," replies Rosemary, suggesting Crimson returns inside. "I must take my hat off to you, Primrose. I admire your courage. This visit must be difficult for you, casting aside our differences to make the first move."

"Let's not get carried away, Rosemary," states Primrose, sternly and impatiently. "You know why I am here."

"And why's that, Primrose?" toys Rosemary, relishing every second to see her rival slither and squirm, then pushing her luck, "Come to buy a bouquet of Lancaster red roses?"

"Absolutely, not!" responds Primrose, admitting defeatedly, "I want to taste your bloody red chocolate!"

"Why didn't you say?" says Rosemary, knowingly, like the cat that got the cream. "It will be my pleasure to show you around and serve you a mug of our finest hot red chocolate. Come with me, Primrose. Into the devil's den!"

Primrose reluctantly follows Rosemary's footsteps, skipping the queue to upstairs, the sound of the chocolate waterfall increasing with every riser.

Then, like a sensory overload, the smell and the sight of chocolate, fuse with sound and motion, controlled by a constant red glow, illuminating the heart and the brain simultaneously. Primrose stands speechless, understanding why Pearl insisted she experiences this spectacle for herself.

Intrigued, Primrose reaches for the waterfall, banging her knuckles on the glass screen, immediately turning to hide embarrassment and avert to the central viewing area.

"Which flavour would you like?" asks Rosemary, handing Primrose a red menu card showing five distinctive choices. "I recommend the strawberry honey and nutmeg."

Primrose reads aloud, "One, lavender-scented burnt caramel. Two, strawberry honey and nutmeg. Three, red-hot chilli Brazil nut crunch. Four, lemon, lime and liquorice, star anise. Five, raspberry-red, orange-amber and mint-green traffic light surprise."

"Or you can gamble your luck," dares Rosemary, handing Primrose a single red die covered in gold spots. "And leave it to chance."

"But there are only five flavours," puzzles Primrose, studying the die. "What if you throw a six?"

"Then your drink is free, and you roll again," reveals Rosemary, delighting in her generosity. "But don't worry, Primrose. This one's on me!"

"Nice touch, Rosemary!" acknowledges Primrose, throwing the die on the long red felt board simulating casino craps, shouting, "Five, raspberry-red, orange-amber and mint-green traffic light surprise."

Rosemary's new shop assistants, Vermillion, real name, Susan, and Carmine, real name, Jenny, serve Primrose her selected hot chocolate in a rose-shaped red handle-less mug, mercifully cool to the touch. At the same time, Rosemary retrieves a red box of chocolates from the refrigerator display.

Primrose takes a sip, tasting the earthy sweet raspberry drupelets burst with intensity to be replaced by the warmth and citrus sun kiss of orange to finish with a slap on the inside of her cheeks as sharp, refreshing mint cleanses the palette to prepare for the next sip. Dropping her guard, Primrose spills over with enthusiasm. "This is remarkable, Rosemary," immediately turning defensive at the sight of Rosemary smiling smugly, and the thought of customers deserting York Blooms café playing heavily on her mind. "Although I have to say, I still prefer coffee."

"Whatever, Primrose," replies Rosemary, dismissively, handing her the box of chocolates, no longer a peace offering. "You had to be indifferent, didn't you? What is it with you? Is it jealously or darn right pig-headedness?"

"I'm sorry, Rosemary," snaps Primrose, rejecting the box of chocolates as if riddled with the plague. "I wouldn't take your chocolates even if I hadn't eaten for forty days and forty nights, and as for your hot chocolate, you can stick it where the sun don't shine!"

Customers stop in their tracks, mouths aghast, frozen in time to witness such a scene in sleepy old Rosewall.

"I will delight in the demise of insignificant and trivial York Blooms," retaliates Rosemary with gloves off. "Your super safe haven of white. Everything bland, innocuous and boring. Just like you."

"And I will do everything in my powers to unravel your over complacency!" shouts Primrose, heading for the exit and throwing her remaining lukewarm chocolate over the waterfall wall, proclaiming, "At least I don't rely on gimmicks!"

Primrose tears downstairs and out of the House of Lancaster, cursing her decision to come. She resolves there and then to change York blooms to the House of York and to play every marketing trick under the sun to entice back customers.

Rosemary stands flabbergasted, astounded at this unnecessary episode, knowing deep down that she added to it by rubbing Primrose's nose in it a tad too much. "Hot chocolates all round," Rosemary declares, looking apologetically at Vermillion and Carmine before she disappears downstairs. "Hot chocolates on the House of Lancaster."

•

As if the script could not become more complex and absurd, something happens that night to fan the flames of hatred more brightly and drive an even greater wedge between Primrose and Rosemary, cementing the feud between the House of York and the House of Lancaster.

Curiously, the three reservoir tanks in the attic that feed the chocolate waterfall break free from their mounting on the division wall, toppling over like falling trees in a forest. A torrent of warm liquid chocolate sweeps across the attic floor like a destructive tsunami, causing the ceiling to fail, flooding the upper floor of the House of Lancaster, cascading down both stairs and through the central viewing gallery onto the red roses below, before streaming to the front door and seeping out onto the pavement. No longer at liquid temperature, the chocolate solidifies like molten lava, turning everything to stone. What was red is now chocolate coloured albeit the red chocolate colour of the House of Lancaster.

Rosemary stands dumbstruck and inconsolable as Crimson, Vermillion and Carmine try to clean, their brooms no match for this colossal bar of chocolate.

"How could she steep so low?" screams Rosemary, tears raining down both cheeks as she holds a bouquet of red roses, caked in chocolate, unsellable and irretrievable. "Carrying out such an indefensible act of terror when we weren't even able to put up a fight. Naked and defenceless and asleep in our beds."

Without stopping to think or to wait for a proper post-mortem, Rosemary picks up a metal doorstop and marches around to York Blooms. Yet to rename or react to yesterday's incident, Primrose, Pearl and Matt are savouring the first coffee of the day before opening.

Throwing the doorstop through one of the windows, Rosemary screams, "If you think York Blooms can take on the House of Lancaster and get away with it," as Primrose comes outside to confront, "then think again. You're too cowardly and colourless."

"If this is how you react to a mugful of lukewarm chocolate," responds Primrose, staring incredulously at her broken window, without knowledge of the chocolate flood. "Then you need your head testing!"

"I'm going to come back fighting," rants Rosemary, fed up with decades of ill-feeling and resentment. "Bigger and stronger, inventing another Lancaster rose to blow the York rose off the map forever."

"There you go again, Rosemary. As cocky as ever," retorts Primrose, also pushed to her limit. "You will rue the day you took on York Blooms, now the House of York, a force for the future never to be underestimated."

"Whoever wins the best rose at the annual summer fete will take ownership of both florists," gambles Rosemary, hoping to rid Rosewall of Primrose forever. "The other agreeing to hand over the keys outright and never to trade again."

"I accept the challenge," risks Primrose, photographing Rosemary and the broken window on her mobile phone while both sets of employees witness this extreme and life-changing wager. "Now get off my pavement before I call the police."

"With pleasure!" yells Rosemary, already regretting her impulsiveness, screaming again, "With pleasure!"

8
War and peace!

Freckles, GR8 and D8, are lunching undercover at The Ratz, discussing and coordinating tactics for the upcoming Day-V counterattack, selecting this strategic restaurant to track the arrival of Queen V's recently summoned armada. F8 acts as a waiter again, perfecting plate carrying skills and multi-pouring techniques. Freckles wears a red silk headscarf and large dark glasses. GR8 endeavours to fit into civilian clothes, complaining about the lack of table legroom, and moaning at the onset of pins and needles. D8 is impeccably dressed, as usual, continuing to oversee many time zones and to crosscheck timesheets and rosters.

"Compliments to Chef Bray, Kismet," praises Freckles, holding out her glass for F8 to refill. "This maggotto with sautéed worms is spot on."

"Chef Bray will be delighted," replies F8, playing along, not wanting to point out that the sautéed worms are curried caterpillars, tossed in garlic. "Have you heard anything from L8?" F8 whispers discreetly.

"L8 took a task force on night manoeuvres last night and discovered Monarch Madame Butterfly and Red Admiral Napoleon weighing anchor at Portsmush about half a mile downriver," relays Freckles, looking at D8 to expand as she sucks down another caterpillar, slurping and burping. "Goodness, these worms are magnificent!"

"While Monarch Madame Butterfly and Red Admiral Napoleon dined in the hindquarters of their flagship galleon," details D8, downloading photos from L8 and displaying for all to see. "Her army of grenadier frogs were gallivanting with all the flirty frogs onshore and getting into all kinds of compromising positions. Meanwhile, the French hornets were making a right old racket in the port bars, while the red jacket wasps were rampaging and ransacking water loos and resisting arrest by the local woodlice police."

"What a bunch of scallywags," remarks GR8, unimpressed by such ill-discipline. "They probably think it's going to be a walkover, unaware that Riverbanks has built its own armada and is ready and waiting."

"You say that, GR8," responds D8, checking his wristwatches once more. "There must be something wrong with the Wi-Fi. Another message has just come through late from L8, sent with the early morning chorus, describing how Monarch Madame Butterfly is on the move." D8 taps a few sums into the computer, muttering under breath and sighing, "By my calculations, they will be arriving any minute now."

"OMG!" exclaims F8, gazing out of the window across to the river estuary to spot the advance flotilla of frigates sail into view, skippered by various butterflies and moths. "They're here."

"How could we have been caught out so badly?" despairs Freckles, gulping down the last caterpillar as Monarch Madame Butterfly, in all her glory, glides into view at the helm of the grandest warship ever to grace Watermill Stream. "Playing with bowls of food as if we have all the time in the world."

Freckles disappears through a trap door underneath her seat, while GR8, D8 and F8 head for The Ratz jetty where B8 awaits in the speed leaf. They alert Shelduck summer camp as they race back to Riverbanks to sound the alarm, where Rodin is chiselling the final touches to the figurehead of The Bee's Knees, ship-named in recognition of Queen B's love for Buzz and the shape of the frontal battering ram.

The flotilla funnel necks into Watermill stream, spearheading Monarch Madame Butterfly and Red Admiral Napoleon's battleship, *La Revolution*, carrying it to the finish line like a peloton preserving its prime rider. La Revolution is carved from a single oak bough, its figurehead a topless *Liberty*, determined and romantically Delacroix. Caterpillars crawl around the rigging, tying everything in knots and assisting Monarch Madame Butterfly, Red Admiral Napoleon and their team of smaller butterflies to extend their wings for full effect and to present true colours of intimidation and dominance. Monarch Madame Butterfly is wearing red, glowing in the afternoon sun, silhouetted and patterned in black like a Goth's eyeliner. Red Admiral Napoleon dresses in black with a distinctive red marking, shoulder white stripes denoting rank, and a black bicorn hat. Diminutive in size but a brilliant tactician, Red Admiral Napoleon commands and manoeuvres La Revolution to countless victories, despite carrying an incapacitating injury to his port wing. The other butterflies form a tricolour of red, white and blue, some with menacing tattoos, others with prominent battle scars, all contributing to this Gallic galleon of immense strength and power.

The grenadier frogs occupy the lower decks, croaking calls of camaraderie, attended by two-legged tadpole powder monkeys and fire-breathing hawker dragonflies, prepared to pack a punch with a suite of water reed cannons aiming both sides. The French hornets are all hands-on deck in black and yellow hoop shirts of the seven seas with bright yellow bandanas, biting at the bit to jump ship for hand to hand cutlass combat. The red jacket wasps are below deck in hammocks, nursing sore heads, washing and mending uniforms after last night's shenanigans. The plan is to moor just outside the brick arch leading to Watermill Gardens and await further instructions from Queen V.

King Fisher has joined Queen Fishnette, Prince Fishin and Princess Fishelle at Shelduck summer camp to put phase one into action, which also involves Mallard and Eider and their duck school of kayakers.

Filled with renewed vigour to use fishing skills other than to catch fish, Princess Fishelle sits with King Fisher on one side of Watermill Stream, and Prince Fishin accompanies Queen Fishnette opposite, not too far from Shelduck summer camp.

King Fisher and Queen Fishnette cast first, sending a fine fishing line to each other's side, bypassing the water altogether. Prince Fisher and Princess Fishelle connect the hooks to pre-mounted rings held firm in the ground, then cast second as King Fisher and Queen Fishelle hook their lines to create a criss-cross of invisible tripwires in time for the fast-approaching flotilla.

One skipper after other jettisons into the air, crash-landing into their respective dinghies, fashioned from hollowed-out elm branches, now sail-less and drifting chaotically in all directions but forwards. King Fisher, Queen Fishnette, Prince Fishin and Princess Fishelle unhook every line, reeling in to hide any evidence, and leaving the frigate skippers dazed and confused and bedraggled. Monarch Madame Butterfly and Red Admiral Napoleon shout and curse as the convoy dismantles.

Meanwhile, Mallard and Eider launch the follow-up. Armed with weeks of daily practice and hard work, Garganey, Gadwall, Pintail, Shoveler and Wigeon become expert kayakers alongside Teal, Ruddy and Mandarin. Pretending to be novices, they paddle back and forth, innocently splishing and splashing, rocking and rolling, and creating a massive swell to compete with any tidal bore, flooding and capsizing each frigate one by one. The overturned skippers struggle to remain afloat, kicking frantically and trying in vain to butterfly and to elevate their wings, until finally waterlogged, each submerges and disappears from view, carried back towards the river alongside their upturned hulls.

Mallard and Eider pretend to scold the duck school, ordering them back to Shelduck before Monarch Madame Butterfly or Red Admiral Napoleon can counteract, instead, gathering in their sails to halt La Revolution.

King Fisher flies back through the brick arch, signalling phase two. Sheila ties one end of a long rope around her middle and hands the other end to Vince. Inhaling deeply, Sheila swallow dives from the right bank, swimming underwater beneath the brick arch and onto La Revolution where unbeknown, she reef knots the rope to the underside before returning to repeat the procedure several times.

While Sheila catches her breath and basks in a job well done, Daphne, Fred, Vince, Rachael and Roland double-check binds before straddle jumping into Watermill Stream and breast stroking upstream towards Riverbanks. At first, progress seems futile, all five appearing to swim against the tide, King Fisher and the frog and toad dockers screaming encouragement from both banks as if attending a meet. Then slowly but surely, each stroke repays double, dragging La Revolution towards the brick arch.

"Weigh anchor," screams Monarch Madame Butterfly, bemused as to why La Revolution is moving without wind nor sail and about to pass the rendezvous. Somehow, she overlooks to warn Queen V.

"Weigh anchor," repeats Red Admiral Napoleon as a burley caterpillar untethers the anchor to discover that there is no anchor. Sheila shrewdly gnawed through the anchor rope after her third visit, sending the dead weight to bed.

As La Revolution drifts through the brick arch, White Admiral Nelson takes charge of The Bee's Knees, relying less on sail power and more on its ingenious mechanism housed within that transforms running action into propulsion. Bryan and his fellow water boatmen sprint on treadmills to the sound of headphones blaring motivational exercise music to gear several sycamore seeds, cleverly bound together to form a propeller.

Carpenter bees beavered away under direction from Harry and with wood donated by Travis and Purrkins to convert one large beech tree bough and two cherry tree branches into a slimline and modern tri catamaran. The faster the boat goes, the more it lifts out of the water, creating less drag, aided by White Admiral Nelson streamlining the butterfly crew for maximum output. Stealth like and lightweight, The Bee's Knees carries no ammunition nor firepower, its weapon a wood-splitting wedge to deliver the destructive final blow.

Lord and Lady Bird outdo themselves yet again, Lady Bird designing uniforms for White Admiral Nelson, Queen B and the B Team, Lord Bird dressing Colonel Rant and the infantry, and Rob and Bob. White Admiral Nelson has a honey colour tightfitting suit, shimmering and changing tones in the wind, decorated with white epaulettes and a large white chest sash to house a plethora of medals and ribbons and to compliment a white silk-rim honey colour hat.

A war cry sounds out from Dolicho while Dronny and Dyetee catch up on missed sleep. Lennon, Dylan, Thomas and Clarice, perform the Riverbanks Anthem, directing loudspeakers across Watermill Stream to blast the stirring sound for all to hear. They modify the lyrics to suit the occasion and the sensitivities of the late risers and the recently woke.

The frog and toad dockers dive bomb from both banks as Carrie delivers the biggest shockwave, showering La Revolution in streams of water, soaking the gunpowder and extinguishing the dragonfly fire breath, and rendering the sitting duck lame and ineffective. The French hornets have no other ship to jump, and the red jackets are running around in underwear, exposed and vulnerable. Sam and Ella and Tyrol bombard La Revolution with nuts, while Barton and Barbara, Beyoncé and Destiny, launch an aerial attack, dropping pebbles and twigs from on high with devastating results. Sorrow lands the sucker punch with a maggot pie smack in the face of Monarch Madame Butterfly and Red Admiral Napoleon, never expecting such a perfect hit.

Monarch Madame Butterfly and Red Admiral Napoleon are speechless and custard-covered, cowering from the onslaught, unaware that The Bee's Knees slices through the bow, tearing down the statue of Liberty to float away downstream, and cutting La Revolution clean in two. Grenadier frogs flee for their lives, immediately overrun with lethal leg holds from the frog and toad dockers before they have a chance to frog kick away from the wreckage. "Take that, Monsieur Croak," scowls Foreman Frankie, squeezing tighter and tighter around the grenadier captain before serving the final course. "As you Croak, Monsieur!"

Red jacket wasps and French hornets splash around powerlessly, unable to swim, gasping for air as each breath takes on more water, drowning in emotion and drifting into obscurity. Monarch Madame Butterfly and Red Admiral Napoleon cut their losses and rigging to retreat through the brick arch rather than face the humiliation of surrender, leaving the caterpillar crew as easy pickings for Chav and her friends. Dunny, Putz, Bozo and Kwim try to partake in the defeat, more obstructive than helpful, although tweeting more significant input for years to come.

Both halves of La Revolution limp downstream out of sight under the brick arch as Riverbanks erupts into a muted celebration, everyone reining in excitement for fear of alerting Queen V before stage two of the Day-V counterattack commences.

•

In the days leading up to the counterattack, Queen B orders specific preparations to set the scene, leaving no stone unturned within the vicinity of The Barb. Using a combination of S.P.I.N's tunnel network and routine deliveries aboveground, Jack and Jimmy, and Catty and the Caterpillar Caterers deposit and disguise boxfuls of nut bombs, twig grenades, grass spears, stinky poo pellets, and sticky tree sap.

Mumble and Stutter special-brew barrels of super-sweet nectar, placing by well-known wasp landing sites. A crack squad of fireflies and glow-worms raid Dolicho, holding Dronny and Dyetee captive, stripping the liquor store to fill peapods with flammable cocktails and easy-light fuses before storing on B Hive roof in preparation for the B Team drone strike.

Rob and Robyn pretend to move to a new house, building a nest directly beneath The Barb just a few branches down, facilitated by Bob and Bruna to transport materials in record time, usually a gruelling and lengthy process that brings stress and stretches patience to its limit.

Margot and Bullet create clear road markings, mapping the under-apple tree area to coincide with tunnel entrances and escape routes back to Watermill Stream, feeding back to D8 to incorporate into the bigger picture.

The carpenter ants construct an enormous wooden horsefly, beautifully crafted in birch with exquisite delta wings, wheeling the trojant horsefly close to the red apple tree and equipping with enough rations and facilities to house Colonel Rant and the Coolstream infantry within the heart of wasp territory until deployment.

Buddy and Hollie and the Leftside Rockers, together with Mo and the martial artists, and Gordon and fellow stags, vacate Lorna's Diner temporarily and frequent Tally's Milk and Honey

Bar. Run by an ageing adder, Tally's is a hip joint in Lancaster garden, once a favourite of the Rightside Mods, now a regular haunt for those down on luck. Meanwhile, Lorna creates an underground mess ready to feed and water everyone in hours of need. Doctor Ida and Nurse Antonia organise a subterranean hospital, expecting inevitable casualties and possible fatalities. Eartha discovers her calling as an electrician, installing underground lighting to ease navigation through the complex maze of tunnels.

G8 taps into The Barb's computer network, intercepting internal communications and monitoring movement inside and out with the help of CCTV installed by B8.

H8 trains a superior force of elite spiders to disarm three wasps at a time, using a combination of strength and silk spun ties and cuffs.

F8 and R8 continue reconnaissance and surveillance, briefing Queen B and the B team and Colonel Rant and the Coolstream infantry, while L8 operates the nightshift to maintain around the clock observation.

M8 sees more and more of Princess Wasperella, initially extracting information on Day-V, subsequently growing fonder and fonder and falling in love.

•

"I hear that VV is designing state-of-the-art toilets for the headquarters of entrepreneur rabbits, Warren and Hutch," remarks Prince Dauber, catching up on current affairs on his tablet over lunch. At the same time, Queen V reads over briefing notes for Day-V.

"I knew her career would go down the pan after that fiasco with The Barb cladding," responds Queen V, tongue in cheek as in bounces Princess Wasperella. "You seem sprightly for a change, Princess."

"I'm in love!" declares Princess Wasperella, a matter of factly and grinning from ear to ear. "And I want the whole world to know."

"So, who is this love interest?" enquires Queen V, looking at Prince Dauber and rolling her eyes with a sense of déjà vu. "Someone, we know?"

"No one, you know," replies Princess Wasperella, knowing this will annoy her parents and put a spanner in the works.

"I expect it's one of those visiting French hornets," suggests Prince Dauber, disapproving, adding undiplomatically. "Everyone knows what's on their mind...and it's not the solution to world hunger. Unless of course, one refers to an appetite of the insatiable kind. Horny French devils!"

"It could be good for international relations, though," ponders Queen V, talking as if Princess Wasperella is not present. "Better that than the scandal of becoming involved with a common drone."

"Goodness me!" cries Prince Dauber, reading breaking news. "La Revolution has been sunk with Monarch Madame Butterfly and Red Admiral Napoleon abandoning ship and deserting the scene. All onboard drowning or swept away downstream."

"Nonsense," dismisses Queen V in denial. "La Revolution is indestructible, and Monarch Madame Butterfly would never fly the scene and leave us defenceless, although I can't vouch for Red Admiral Napoleon."

"There are pictures from one of the grenadier frogs," replies Prince Dauber, delivering a bombshell. "King Fisher is standing victorious on one half of La Revolution."

"He's a spider!" blurts Princess Wasperella, piggybacking on the timely catastrophe. "His name is Connor Cadd, and we are in love!"

"This is a disaster!" exclaims Queen V, resigned to sacrificing Riverbanks, not knowing whether to look to Prince Dauber for support or to scorn Princess Wasperella for self-interest at a time of colonial crisis. "We have to bring Day-V forwards if we stand any chance of at least beating those blasted bees, and as for being in love with a spider, Wasperella," Queen V protests out of hand. "Over my dead body."

A nut bomb explodes through The Barb roof before Queen V can issue orders, sending everything into pandemonium. Buzz and the B Team drone strike deliver knockout punch after another, causing a mass exodus of yellow jacket drones and workers attempting to re-enact rehearsals, some without time to dress appropriately. The French hornets, calm and collected, arm to the hilt, anger growing with added venom.

Princess Wannabee leads the B Team workers, transformed into a mean machine, waiting underground and wearing black and gold lycra tight-fitting jumpsuits with integral armour and reinforced wings.

"All systems go," G8 communicates by earpieces to everyone on B Team and joined by Queen B and Freckles in the underground control room, feet from the action. "Go, H8. Go."

H8 and the elite squad take the left side of the red apple tree, disarming and detaining yellow jacket after yellow jacket as if on a Sunday stroll. M8 and B8 tag along for the simple ride.

"Princess Wannabee and the B Team workers. Go," continues G8, glancing several monitors in tandem.

Princess Wannabee and the B Team workers emerge from the tunnel to take the centre-ground, confronting unsuspecting yellow jackets, most more interested in the barrels of available special brew after Mumble and Stutter swoop to remove the lids. Queen V and Princess Wasperella observe from the balcony of The Barb as the B Team entrap yellow jackets in sticky tree sap, pelt with stinky poo pellets, and knock out with nut bombs, twig grenades and grass spears.

"Colonel Rant and the Coolstream infantry. Go," commands G8, releasing the trapdoor within the trojant horsefly.

One by the one, the infantry, barely fighting age, some distinctly juvenile and pushing luck, climb down to attack from behind. "Charge!" bawls Colonel Rant, leading by example, relying on strength in numbers and overpowering the enemy with collective force, stripping both the dignity and the yellow jacket clothing of disarmed victims before carrying aloft and discharging ungraciously in a growing pile beneath the red apple tree.

"Buddy, Hollie and the crickets. Go. Mo and the martial artists. Go. Gordon and fellow stags. Go," orchestrates G8, pointing at the screens like a conductor, swept away in the music of madness.

Exiting Tally's, a gang of French hornets are waiting, as if anticipating a move on the right flank. Tally bolts doors and boards up her bar, too accustomed to previous events that quickly get out of hand. Gordon and the other stags appear to hold their own, using a steady stock of pebbles and twigs to clean and jerk before propelling towards the advancing foe, flattening like dominoes. Mo and the martial artists, karate kick and punch the opposition, mesmerising with quick reactions and superfast strikes, swerving any sword advances to rotate and land a fatal head blow, always ending in prayer and ironic anguish.

Buddy and Hollie and the crickets come out fighting but soon find they are no match for the superior size and strength of the French hornets. However much they dance side to side and move and shake hips to avoid stabbing thrusts, the hornets play by different rules, doubling up and attacking from all sides. Hollie finds herself cornered as three French hornets come in for the kill. Buddy throws himself in the firing line, managing to swerve initial advances until he mistimes to a steel shaft stabbing into his abdomen and carving up his insides, embedding a paralysing and painful sting. "Buddy," screams Hollie as Gordon and two other stags come to her rescue.

"I'm Okay," mutters Buddy, bravely, unaware of the blood pouring from his open gut, the blade still wedged deep and impossible to remove. "Just help me up. Let's finish this rumble."

"Oh, Buddy," cries Hollie, watching the music die as he slips in and out of consciousness before closing his eyes and exhaling his final breath, his body slumping lifelessly in her arms.

Hollie cannot muster words, only heart-stabbing hurt.

Queen B witnesses the brutal and callous death of Buddy as Hollie kneels by his side, sobbing and begging the cricket gods to extend his innings. Queen B has no choice but to serve poetic justice, ordering Dylan and Thomas to ignite Rob and Robyn's new nest to wipe clean the smile from the face of Queen V as she stands smug in her ivory paper tower.

The nest sparks into life, creating an immediate funeral pyre as flames fan higher and higher towards the underside of the Barb. Queen V and Princess Wasperella are about to fly the coop when flames rip up one side of The Barb, entrapping both and sealing their fate. "CONNOR," screams Princess Wasperella as an ultimate declaration of love and despair.

M8 hears Princess Wasperella name-call his alias, igniting an inner passion and a belief that nothing else matters but to save his beloved. Leaving H8, B8 and the elite squad to work through the continual onslaught of one yellow jacket line after another, M8 scales the red apple tree, swinging from branch to branch and pulling up on silk spun ropes before arriving at the balcony.

Luckily, M8's combat suit is fire retardant and with all arms, succeeds in dislodging one burning section to fall through the apple tree like dripping embers through a fire hearth, reaching through to grab Princess Wasperella. "Mother!" she yells as M8 holds her tightly and whispers, "I've got you, Princess."

M8 extends another arm and manages to locate Queen V, reeling in just in time to abseil away from the balcony as wildfire spreads and illuminates The Barb like an oriental lantern. They land at the bottom of the apple tree to confront more carnage as the battle rages all about.

"Mother, meet Connor," shouts Princess Wasperella, picking a bizarre moment while she hugs Queen V. "The spider I love and who saved your life," turning to kiss M8 and to thank for rescuing them both. "And Connor, meet my mother. Matriarch and ruler of the wasps. Queen V."

Meanwhile, Buzz goes in for one last strike as yellow jacket drones begin to strike back, dogfighting B team drones, occasionally direct hitting to send crash-landing to earth. Prince Dauber sees a perfect chance and sets all targets on Buzz, weaving and swaying until sights lock, launching a missile that wings Buzz and sends him into an uncontrolled spin. Realising that any attempt to return to B Hive is inconceivable, Buzz has no other choice but to emergency land close to Princess Wannabee, Prince Dauber hot on his heels and determined to put an end to this formidable talisbee.

Buzz scrapes along the ground, falling head over heels and scraping knees and arms before coming to a stop, semi-conscious and severely damaged. Prince Dauber places a left knee on the throat of Buzz, incapacitating and slowly sucking the life.

Queen B has seen enough, watching everything unfold in graphic detail. She abandons the monitoring station and heads above ground, exiting the tunnel in the proximity of Princess Wannabee, pleading anxiously, "Enough is enough, Prince Dauber, spelt E_N_O_U_G_H. Let Buzz go, spelt G_O."

Prince Dauber ignores Queen B, applying more pressure and looking to Queen V for a turned thumb and *coup de grâce*, like a victorious gladiator in the Coliseum.

"Please, Queen V, spelt P_L_E_A_S_E," begs Queen B, seeing the colour drain from Buzz's face as he hangs onto life with failing fingertips. "What has Buzz ever done to you, spelt Y_O_U?"

"She's right, mother," agrees Princess Wasperella, overstepping into unchartered territory. "You have the power to end all this misery. To set a future that's bright and beautiful rather than burdened with hatred and misery."

"Wasperella's right. Do we have to spell it out for you?" aligns Princess Wannabee, pointing at Hollie holding Buddy's dead body before staring at both Queens intensely. "There has to be more to life than nectar and honey. Surely, there's a way to work together and to distribute resources fairly and squarely so that everyone can live in harmony, enjoying rather than fearing life?"

"I'm happy to back down if you back down, Queen V, spelt B_A_C_K_D_O_W_N," concedes Queen B, smiling at Princess Wannabee and Princess Wasperella for speaking their mind and for sounding sense, desperate to save Buzz and pursue peace rather than mortal combat. "What do you say, Queen V, spelt S_A_Y?"

"Please, mother," Princess Wasperella begs once more. "Connor just saved your life. Surely that counts for something?"

"Very well, Queen B," accepts Queen V after what seems a lifetime, gesturing for Prince Dauber to release the grip on Buzz. "Let's end this pointless destruction and bloodshed and create a better community where something other than nectar and honey makes the world go around."

Both Queens order a ceasefire, Queen B rushing to aid Buzz, and calling on Rob and Bob to extinguish The Barb as Barton and Barbara assist in dropping buckets of steam water from on high, managing to save the majority for another day. Unfortunately, it does not undo the death count strewn around the spent battlefield, a harsh reminder of blind loyalty and misconceptions of grandeur.

Bodies are buried where fallen, ceremoniously covered in red and white rose petals as a sign of unity and respect. Dylan and Thomas bugle *The Last Post* in moments of silence and reflection as the late afternoon sun casts long shadows, emphasizing how far everyone has come and yet how far there is to go.

"About my name," M8 confesses to Princess Wasperella, sheepishly, as they retire to the makeshift underground camp. "My name's not Connor. I am an undercover Spyder working for S.P.I.N with the code name, M8, and that's my boss, Freckles," pointing at Freckles dressed in a pink apron, helping Lorna, Queen B and Queen V to dish out evening rations with a healthy portion of humble pie.

"Connor, M8, Spyder, S.P.I.N, blah, blah, blah!" proclaims Princess Wasperella on cloud nine, "All I know is that we make each other happy and we're supposed to be together. I don't care about any of that mumbo jumbo. You're my perfect mate, M8!"

"A spider and a wasp. Who'd have thought it possible?" ponders M8, holding his Princess aloft before wrapping her finger with silk thread and tying the knot. "How crazy is that!"

9
Peace and harmony and two doors!

Primrose and Rosemary have no interaction since that fateful day when chocolate almost brought unity, ironically driving them further apart. It is unproblematic to continue separate lives with independent doors to both the florists and the cottages. The decking fence may as well be ten-foot-tall and three-foot-thick when there is no desire to communicate even if curiosity occasionally rears its ugly head. Should they exit or enter their cottages coincidentally, one or other conveniently forget something inside or remain at the wheel, engrossed in a mobile phone or an out of date pamphlet.

Watermill gardens hibernate during the winter. The odd chirping robin or blackbird landing close to the decking acts as a reminder that everything is just dormant. Primrose and Rosemary spend inordinate amounts of time in their respective potting sheds, converting determination into dedication in search of the holy grail and an answer to silence their side thorns forever. Come spring, both erect screens behind which they plant sufficient quantities of selected succulents to more than satisfy entry to the annual summer fete.

The House of Lancaster continues to thrive with its restored chocolate café, additional media coverage of the *chocolate disaster,* adding to its notoriety and outreach. The resultant global customer base, online and anonymous, is desperate to form an opinion on the latest *must-have* and to join in the frenzy of posting more and more outrageous locations and pouted positions for eating red chocolate, the outcomes best left to the imagination. Rosemary ignores the insurance report that highlights an installation fault, refusing an apology to Primrose, saving face to continue her family legacy to do away with any York claim and to put an end this eternal feud once and for all.

Meanwhile, Primrose relaunches as the House of York, promoting a competitive range of white chocolate. The sculpted pentagon bars resemble the York white rose with an additional golden hub of solidified *honey from heaven* and packaged in a white five-sided box, sold individually or in quantities of three, six, nine and twelve. Customers create hot chocolate at the York café by merely dropping a single five-segment rose into a mug containing correct measures of milk and water, and heating over a specially designed tabletop coaster. Coffee and tea still prevail alongside hot chocolate to endorse *own-brewing* and the rechargeable York Coaster device, portable, convenient and internet bestseller, also reaching a global audience beyond the wildest imagination of Rosewall.

Strangely, the York white rose makes a resurgence over the winter as the go-to flower, exampling how fickle and unpredictable fashion can be. There are no chocolate waterfalls or other eye-catching gimmicks, just simplicity personified, although it must be said that white chocolate is not to all tastes.

•

The morning of the annual summer fete begins like any other morning with Primrose sipping tea on her deck and Rosemary still to rise. Except for today, unlike last year, the weather is unkind, casting doubt and jeopardy over many of the outside events, forecasting heavy rain with possible thunderstorms. Luckily, the best rose competition is inside. Noticeably, rather like humans, flowers react to the conditions, wilting when experiencing bouts of depression or performing better under high pressure. Primrose sings her words of encouragement but sighs defeat as if struggling in vain to entice a teenager from its bed. She studies her new bloom, a creation beyond her wildest dreams that will surely sink Rosemary and inherit the House of Lancaster, even go down in history as the first of its kind and to carry her name in stone.

Meanwhile, Pearl, Matt and new addition, Ivory arrive early at the village green to create the York white chocolate café in a prime spot within the marquee, publicising the House of York by selling the York Coaster at a discount for all those presenting a valid loyalty card.

Unsurprisingly, Crimson, Vermillion and Carmine are directly opposite, operating the Lancaster red chocolate café, promoting the House of Lancaster with half-price chocolates, kept cool in refrigerator displays.

It is dark red chocolate versus white chocolate, and red rose set against white rose, the House of Lancaster anti the House of York, one looking to reign supreme, unable to coexist or incorporate contrast and diversity. An either-or, never together. Most customers are oblivious, happy to indulge and make room in their hearts and minds for both, as natural as night follows day, and death ends life.

Primrose defers cutting as long as she can, then wearing white gloves, she delicately secateurs two dozen stems into a House of York white flower carrier. She transfers immediately to her van alongside a novel vase design and a flower care kit containing moisturising spray, flower feed and display accessories. Eager not to reveal her entry before judging nor to catch a glimpse of Rosemary's beady eye, Primrose takes a circular white screen.

Rosemary, safe in the knowledge that Primrose will arrive with too much time to fill, allows another hour or so of precious growth for her new rose creation, nurtured with love over many months and brimming with confidence to bring down the House of York. If truth be told, Rosemary is awaiting delivery of a metal display, supposed to arrive yesterday, the maker ringing at the eleventh hour to request more time!

Similar to last year, the only other entry to the rose competition is another hand-picked bouquet from Henry Stafford, another year older and as it appears, another year wiser. Taking inspiration and the flowers from the Woodville Castle wall, Henry arranges a rainbow arch of red, white, blue, orange and pink roses. They radiate from a dark green ceramic vase, handmade in school pottery class and complete with fired fingerprints.

Primrose arranges her roses in two concentric pentagon rows around a central flower into sunken silver test tubes, totalling twenty-one magnificent blooms, opening fuller with every gulp of flower feed. The stems sprout from a sizeable triangular tabletop wedge, handcrafted and whitewashed in English oak to display the bouquet purposely at forty-five degrees. A silver plaque engraved with *The House of York Rose* is the final touch of class. Satisfied, Primrose applies the circular screen, closing its concertina. She whispers a prayer, finger-crossing as she places her fate firmly in the lap of the judges.

On the subject of the judges, rumours are rife about bribery and possible retainers, even a seat on the board, and going as far as hands in marriage. The local press is having a village field day, filling column after column with speculation, tittle-tattle and several quotes from distant school friends hellbent on cashing in fifteen minutes of fame. Consequently, the judging panel remains unspecified until the day, villagers wondering whether they will be local or from afar. Either way, this is the most excitement in Rosewall since the theft of the village pub sign, many years ago.

Uncannily, Rosemary arranges her roses in a similar pattern to Primrose, except shooting from a red ceramic bullet-shaped vase, held in a metal hoop at forty-five degrees to a vertical metal pole. The pole spikes into the ground, cantilevering a large circular rail up high for a plush red velvet curtain to enrobe the bouquet in waiting. The metal pole is bright chrome with an inscription plate, etched with *The House of Lancaster Rose*. The similarities are strikingly similar but dramatically different, both raising their game to match the increased stakes, but none the wiser, the entries hiding from view, except that of Henry, the heir apparent and future successor.

The rain is unforgiving, drowning out the tug of war, flattening any hope of the uncoordinated bicycle ride, and transforming the furthest welly into the furthest gym shoe, all wellies fully employed and accounted. Umbrellas make an unexpected comeback. Sausages, yellow plastic ducks and watered-down beverages are more popular than ever, carrying the village through the afternoon and into the marquee for the award ceremony climax. Just as the wind picks up and the clouds darken, and the rain turns to hail, driving golf balls onto the marquee roof like a percussionist boiling a kettle drum, swamping any chit chat. The tension escalates, at least within the hearts of the entrants, specifically, Primrose and Rosemary, again standing apart next to their respective cafes, both a bundle of butterflies and facing Domesday.

With hindsight rather than foresight, the air conditioning unit adds to the chill until Lady Beaufort instructs its demise as goose pimples shiver up and down her spine. The marquee flashes for a split-second, silencing the crowd into counting elephants, awaiting the inevitable thunder toll barely past the strike of six. The villagers scream and cheer simultaneously, quickly changing to laughter and swapping overexcited glances like extras in a second-rate horror movie after the director shouts cut.

"Welcome to the annual summer fete award ceremony," announces Lady Margaret Beaufort in a voice more plummy and fortissimo to be heard. There is a distinct feeling of déjà vu as she taps the microphone to ensure that it is working after noting several members of the audience again cupping their ears. "Can everyone hear me?" she asks, turning to the vicar who nods his head and warms his dog collar with a black scarf.

"Just like last year, there are four categories," outlines Lady Beaufort, revealing four sealed envelopes like a deck of cards. "Best cake. Best pie. Best jam. And best rose.

"As everyone is aware, and if they are not, then where have they been for the last six months?!" jokes Lady Beaufort, smirking at Primrose and Rosemary, then diverting her gaze over her glasses at the local reporter with a phone, poised to capture the moment of truth. "The best rose category will not only decide this year's best rose in Rosewall but also determine whether Lancaster or York Blooms continues to trade, the defeated florist resigning and hanging up their secateurs and wellies forever!"

Primrose simultaneously point at their café namesakes, forcing Lady Beaufort to correct. "My mistake, ladies and gentlemen, today will determine whether the House of Lancaster or the House of York will survive to grow another day."

The audience mutters and mumbles, looking from Primrose to Rosemary, back to Lady Beaufort, almost pleading for an end to this petty feud. The marquee flashes once more, thunder crashing like a Rank Gong at the count of five, the eye of the storm and its strengthening deluge seeping through straining seams, everyone wondering how safe it is to be inside a canvas tent.

"For the sake of fairness and the protection of the individuals," continues Lady Beaufort, injecting further suspense like a murder mystery tour, "the judging panel will remain anonymous. However, the vicar informs me that the judges wish to commend all entrants for raising the bar yet again, making it nigh on impossible to pick a winner, leading to some shock results!"

The marquee flickers like a loose connection, thunder clapping at the count of four. Lady Beaufort cowers behind the microphone, stepping back from the possible conducting rod, eager to conclude all ceremonies.

"The winner of best cake goes to," Lady Beaufort breaks the seal to remove the handwritten note and reads, "Surprise, surprise, or rather no surprise, Mrs Stanley and her magnificent *Egyptian Pharaoh cake.*"

Mrs Stanley walks up to receive a golden rosette and a gift token for the local brasserie, fast becoming a familiar haunt. The local reporter takes a photo, the phone flash disguising the lightning, until thunder booms at the count of three, everyone jumping from their skin.

"Best pie goes to," Lady Beaufort opens the second envelope to read after raising her eyebrows, "Anne Neville, for her mammoth Moby Dick pie, I am sure giving Mr Hastings a run for his money."

The same group of teenagers scream and shout Anne's name, jostling her to the front to collect the golden rosette and a gift voucher for Mr Hastings' fishmongers. Mr Hastings puts on a brave face while the reporter's phone flash acts as a precursor to the lightning, thunder punching at the count of two.

"Now to the award for best jam," continues Lady Beaufort, opening the third envelope and leaning tentatively into the microphone. "Well, this is quite a turnaround. The best jam goes to Mr Hastings and his *fish in a jam*," applauds Lady Beaufort as Mr Hastings comes up to receive a golden rosette and a voucher to the luxury hotel. "You have to try it, ladies and gentlemen. It sounds dubious, but the taste is quite brilliant, albeit for those with stronger morning constitutions!"

The reporter takes a photo, the flash fooling everyone, lightning striking moments later, thunder exploding at the count of one, everyone huddling closer together.

"And now for Rosewall's answer to a soap opera, and the winner of the best rose, and the right to run the only village florists," introduces Lady Beaufort, beginning to open the envelope as the vicar walks over and whispers in her ear. "The judges suggest that the audience view the three entries before announcing the winner. "This is Henry Stafford's entry," begins Lady Beaufort, praising his effort, "a familiar favourite and the Rosewall rainbow."

Then Lady Beaufort draws back Primrose's first-time screening. "Wow! I have never seen anything like it," describes Lady Beaufort as the audience stretches and contorts to sneak a view. "beautifully presented to reveal a red rose outer, encompassing a white heart inner."

Primrose crosses arms, her own heart missing a beat with anxiety. Rosemary stands flabbergasted as Lady Beaufort draws back the red curtain, uncloaking her entry to exclaim, "Wow, again! Is this some sort of joke?"

The audience gasps stunned into silence as they study Primrose's unique flower then Rosemary's distinctive bloom as if looking in a mirror, both flowers identical in every way.

"And on this bombshell," declares Lady Beaufort, pulling out the notelet and reading to herself before reading aloud, "the winner... or should I say winners, are the House of York and the House of Lancaster. A tie."

Lightning direct strikes the central marquee pillar, splitting it in two to a cacophony of noise as the canvas roof rips. Drenching and sending the crowd into chaos, to escape via the nearest exits, stampeding and trampling the odd faller, screaming and giving the thunder a run for its money.

Primrose and Rosemary remain glued to the spot in shock, staring incredulously at each other's entry, shaking heads at the judges' joint decision, neither knowing how to react. Then, as if some puppeteer conducts, they rotate heads to look at each other like a game of who blinks first. Both burst into uncontrolled laughter, tiptoeing towards each other just as the rain miraculously gives way to a beam of sunlight, illuminating their handshake which rapidly transforms into a hug.

"It's a sign, Rosemary," says Primrose, superstitiously.

"A sign from our forefathers," adds Rosemary, nodding at the absurdity of recent events.

"As far back as Edward Windsor," continues Primrose.

"To unite us with one rose," expands Rosemary, making a rose shape with her hands, "by taking the passion and fire of the red rose."

"And wrapping it around the pure heart and goodness of the white rose," details Primrose, placing her fist inside Rosemary's cupped hands. "Working together in total harmony."

"Not joining red and white to make pink," dismisses Rosemary, critically, "that interferes with the whole identity and waters down both offers."

"But to combine the complementary strengths and potency of both signatures, undiluted and instantly recognisable," summarises Primrose, the pair turning to smile for the reporter, who is determined to capture the truce for posterity and the paper, posting online before Primrose and Rosemary consent to their poutless pose!

•

Thankfully there are no casualties following the thunder strike, other than the abandoned entries, now sights for sore eyes. After clearing away both cafés, Primrose and Rosemary invite both sets of employees back to Watermill for a barbecue and a celebratory drink. Mr Hyde reverts to Dr Jekyll as blue sky replaces grey and the evening sun towel dries everything in its path.

Pearl, Matt and Ivory follow Primrose into York Cottage while Crimson, Vermillion and Carmine enter Lancaster Cottage after Rosemary, everyone convening on the rear decking.

"The first thing we need to do, Primrose," shouts Rosemary from behind the fence.

"Is what?" responds Primrose, struggling to hear.

"Is tear this bloody wall down!" yells Rosemary, disappearing inside to fetch a power screwdriver. "You hold your side, and I'll unscrew the brackets on this side."

Rosemary passes the screwdriver over the fence like an illegal transaction or a parcel of hope. Primrose unscrews her brackets then eight pairs of legs frogmarch the wooden panel down to Rosemary's sidewall entrance. Shining axe in hand, they demolish to feed the late evening firepit.

As everyone sits with a plateful of barbecued red and white meat and non-meat, accompanying sumptuous green salads, and holding a glass of their favourite red or white wine tipple, the conversation turns to the future.

"Now that neither House is closing," starts Rosemary to raucous cheers, "perhaps we should think about joining forces."

"Excellent idea," agrees Primrose, lifting her glass in recognition. "To reinstate both florists as one like it used to be."

"Doing away with the division wall," suggests Rosemary, obsessed with tearing down barriers, operating the power screwdriver for robotic effect.

"Combining both cafés on the second floor," details Primrose.

"Selling both York white chocolate and Lancaster red chocolate," says Pearl, looking at Matt and licking her lips at the prospect of easy access to luscious red chocolate.

"Placing the white chocolate rose within the red chocolate flower," suggests Crimson, hoping not to overstep the mark with Rosemary, who smiles back approvingly. "Changing the box packaging to contain a white circle on the upper surface."

"And we can move the chocolate waterfall to the sidewall and replace its inner section with white chocolate," proposes Rosemary, miming her vision. "Red chocolate, white chocolate, red chocolate."

"Like a white rose between two thorns!" jokes Primrose, grinning.

"Or the weaker rose defended by the stronger!" heckles Primrose, also grinning.

"And sell both red and white roses," continues Matt, diverting back to safe ground, looking to Vermillion and Carmine for support.

"And don't forget the new rose," reminds Ivory, everyone agreeing and reliving the earlier fiasco.

Vermillion and Carmine describe Lady Beaufort's fall from grace, as she lands flat on her face in the mayhem, covering her cream outfit from head to toe in dark wet mud, and then watching the vicar follow suit.

"How do you think you came up with the same rose?" continues Ivory, not wanting to appear foolish.

"That's an excellent question, Ivory," replies Rosemary, putting her at ease. "I do recall a couple of bumblebees in the potting shed that must have cross-contaminated the succulents, transferring red pollen to Primrose's shed and white pollen to mine."

"What are the chances of that?" responds Ivory, rhetorically, shaking her head incredulously.

"Talking of the new rose," prompts Primrose, pointing to a vase containing three leftovers. "What are we going to call it?"

"The House of Lancaster York?" suggests Rosemary, provocatively.

"You mean the House of York Lancaster?" corrects Primrose, everyone shifting uncomfortably in their seats, despairing at the feud rekindling.

"If we are uniting both shops back to one," interjects Crimson, diffusing the issue, "then why don't we call it the *two-door rose*, in recognition of the two-door access and the combining of two Houses?"

"Exactly, Crimson!" assists Matt, trying to be helpful. "Every house has a front door. So, two houses have two doors."

"It's as they say," contributes Pearl, injecting humour. "When one door closes, two doors open!"

"We can always rely on your pearls of wisdom, Pearl!" quips Primrose before clarifying the crucial factors. "The Two-door Rose in the Two-door House. I like it."

"The Two-door Rose in the House of Two-door," rearranges Rosemary, smiling favourably at Primrose, everyone unanimous. "Also selling Lancaster red roses and York white roses and Two-door chocolates."

"And Two-door rosé!" adds Vermillion, topping up her red wine with white wine for comedic effect.

"Then it's agreed," concludes Primrose, standing to raise a glass. "Please be upstanding to toast, peace and harmony and the Two-door Rose!" everyone repeating, "Peace and harmony and the Two-door Rose!"

HUMANKIND

Anne Neville	student
Carmine/Jenny	Lancaster Blooms assistant
Crimson	Lancaster Blooms assistant
Ivory	York Blooms assistant
Lady Margaret Beaufort	dignitary
Matt White	York Blooms assistant
Mr Hastings	fishmonger
Mrs Stanley	librarian
Pearl White	York Blooms assistant
Primrose York/White Wellies	York Blooms owner
Redmond	architect
Rosemary Lancaster/Red Wellies	Lancaster Blooms owner
Stanley Thomas	farmer
Vermillion/Susan	Lancaster Blooms assistant

ANIMAL KINGDOM

Antonia	nurse ant	Coolstream	soldier ants
B8	spider	D8	spider
Barbara	crow	Daphne	dormouse
Barton	crow	Destiny	raven
Beyoncé	raven	Dingy Skipper	butterfly
Billie	millipede	Doctor Ida	spider
Bob	blackbird	Dunny	great tit
Bozo	blue tit	Dyetee	wasp
Bray	duck	Dylan	dragonfly
Bruna	blackbird	Eartha	earthworm
Bryan	water boatman	Eider	duck
Buddy	cricket	Ella	harvest mouse
Bullet	slug	F8/Kismet	spider
Buzz	bee	Foreman Frankie	frog
Carrie	bullfrog	Freckles	mole
Catty	caterpillar	Fred	field mouse
Chav	chaffinch	G8	spider
Clarice	starling	Gadwall	duck
Colonel Rant	soldier ant	Garganey	duck

ANIMAL KINGDOM

Gordon	stag beetle	Princess Fishelle	kingfisher
GR8	daddy-long-legs	Princess Wannabee	bee
H8	spider	Princess Wasperella	wasp
Harriet	hummingbird	Purrkins	wood pigeon
Harry	hedgehog	Putz	great tit
Hettie	hummingbird	Queen Abeille/B	bee
Hollie	cricket	Queen Fishnette	kingfisher
Jack	sparrow	Queen Vespula/V	wasp
Jimmy	sparrow	R8	spider
King Fisher	kingfisher	Rachael	brown rat
Kwim	yellow-bellied tit	Red Adm Napoleon	butterfly
Lady Bird	ladybird	Rob	robin
Leftside Rockers	crickets	Robyn	robin
Lenin	ant	Rodin	woodpecker
Lennon	long nose beetle	Roland	brown rat
Lettice	slug	Ruddy	duck
Lord Bird	ladybird	Sam	squirrel
Lorna	grass snake	Serjeant Hill	soldier ant
Lucky	horseshoe bat	Sheila	pygmy shrew
Luther	ant	Shoveler	duck
Lynn	brown rat	Sorrow	magpie
M8/Connor Cadd	spider	Spit	bee
Mallard	drake	Stutter	bumblebee
Mandarin	duck	Tally	adder
Margot	snail/escargot	Teal	duck
Martial artists	grasshoppers	The Scarab Prince	scarab beetle
Mike	money spider	Thomas	dragonfly
Millie	millipede	Travis	wood pigeon
Mitch	brown rat	Twatt	cockroach
Mo	grasshopper	Twitt	cockroach
Monarch Madame	butterfly	Twott	cockroach
Monsieur Croak	frog	Tyrol	squirrel
Mumble	bumblebee	Vespa Velutina	wasp
Pintail	duck	Vince	water vole
Polish	bee	White Adm Nelson	butterfly
Prince Dauber	wasp	Wigeon	duck
Prince Fishin	kingfisher	Willy	woodlouse

THANK YOU FOR READING

I HOPE YOU ENJOYED AS MUCH AS I ENJOYED WRITING

THE WARS OF THE ROSES!

GAVIN THOMSON

BOOKS BY GAVIN THOMSON

JOANNA AND THE PIANO

ISAAC AND NEWTON'S APPLES

PENNY AND THE FARTHING

SNOWBALLS

TWINNING TALES SHORT STORIES

MMXX

I

Printed in Great Britain
by Amazon